The Lawman's Christmas Wish

Linda Goodnight

Published by Steeple Hill Books™

If you purchased this book without a cover you should be aware that this book is stolen property. It was reported as "unsold and destroyed" to the publisher, and neither the author nor the publisher has received any payment for this "stripped book."

Special thanks and acknowledgment to Linda Goodnight for her contribution to the Alaskan Bride Rush miniseries.

STEEPLE HILL BOOKS

Recycling programs
for this product may
not exist in your area.

ISBN-13: 978-0-373-87638-9

THE LAWMAN'S CHRISTMAS WISH

Copyright © 2010 by Harlequin Books S.A.

All rights reserved. Except for use in any review, the reproduction or utilization of this work in whole or in part in any form by any electronic, mechanical or other means, now known or hereafter invented, including xerography, photocopying and recording, or in any information storage or retrieval system, is forbidden without the written permission of the editorial office, Steeple Hill Books, 233 Broadway, New York, NY 10279 U.S.A.

This is a work of fiction. Names, characters, places and incidents are either the product of the author's imagination or are used fictitiously, and any resemblance to actual persons, living or dead, business establishments, events or locales is entirely coincidental.

This edition published by arrangement with Steeple Hill Books.

® and TM are trademarks of Steeple Hill Books, used under license. Trademarks indicated with ® are registered in the United States Patent and Trademark Office, the Canadian Trade Marks Office and in other countries.

www.SteepleHill.com

Printed in U.S.A.

"Sit still for two minutes, relax and drink that cider," Reed said.

"Or what? You gonna arrest me?" Before Ben's death, she and Reed had been good friends. The ill-begotten marriage proposal had raised a hedge between them and Amy missed the silly give-and-take they'd once shared.

At her cheekiness, Reed grinned. Breath clogged in Amy's chest. He scowled and grumbled at her so much, she'd forgotten about his killer grin.

"Could be."

"What's the charge?" she asked.

"Resisting an officer. Disturbing the peace."

"Whose peace am I disturbing?"

His eyes narrowed into slits, but the dark brown irises twinkled. "Mine."

Alaskan Bride Rush:
Women are flocking to the Land of the Midnight Sun with marriage on their minds

Klondike Hero—Jillian Hart
July 2010

Treasure Creek Dad—Terri Reed
August 2010

Doctor Right—Janet Tronstad
September 2010

Yukon Cowboy—Debra Clopton
October 2010

Thanksgiving Groom—Brenda Minton
November 2010

The Lawman's Christmas Wish—Linda Goodnight
December 2010

Books by Linda Goodnight

Love Inspired

In the Spirit of...Christmas
A Very Special Delivery
**A Season for Grace*
**A Touch of Grace*
**The Heart of Grace*
Missionary Daddy
A Time to Heal
Home to Crossroads Ranch
The Baby Bond
***Finding Her Way Home*
***The Wedding Garden*
The Lawman's Christmas Wish

*The Brothers' Bond
**Redemption River

LINDA GOODNIGHT

Winner of a RITA® Award for excellence in inspirational fiction, Linda Goodnight has also won a Booksellers' Best, ACFW Book of the Year and a Reviewers' Choice Award from *RT Book Reviews*. Linda has appeared on the Christian bestseller list and her romance novels have been translated into more than a dozen languages. Active in orphan ministry, this former nurse and teacher enjoys writing fiction that carries a message of hope and light in a sometimes dark world. She and her husband, Gene, live in Oklahoma. Readers can write to her at linda@lindagoodnight.com, or c/o Steeple Hill Books, 233 Broadway, Suite 1001, New York, NY 10279.

And whatsoever ye do, do it heartily,
as to the Lord, and not unto men.
—*Colossians* 3:23

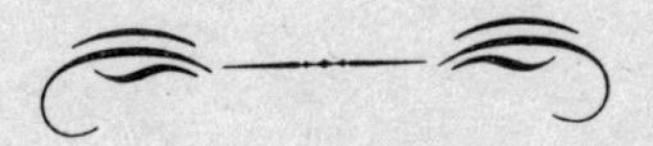

For Maria Masha with love

Chapter One

"You might as well give up and marry me, Miss Amy."

Amy James, in the Treasure Creek General Store shopping for milk and bread—a never-ending need with her two sons—looked at the speaker, Myron Scroggins, without a bit of surprise. Lately, no matter where she went someone proposed marriage. The situation had become beyond ridiculous.

"Oh, Myron, you're just after my money," she said, trying to make light of the silly offer. Everyone in the tiny town of Treasure Creek, Alaska, knew her tour business was struggling. During the last few months, business had improved, but it would be another year before she was back on solid footing.

"Now, Miss Amy, you know better."

She did. Myron was one of the good guys. The burly man was also forty years her senior, lived far outside town and was seriously set in his ways. His scraggly beard probably housed a family of mice. He rarely came to town, and then only to collect supplies and hightail it back to his ramshackle cabin.

Carl Branch, a sixtysomething farmer in brown duck coveralls and a feed-store ball cap, came around from behind a stack of horse feed and protested. "Hey, I asked her first!"

Myron's weathered face fell. He looked from Carl to Amy and back. "You did?"

Amy laughed. She couldn't help herself. In an Alaskan town with few women and plenty of men, she'd become a valuable commodity. Some wanted her tour business, and others simply wanted to take care of the young widow whose family had founded this town. This was the case with both Myron and Carl, two older men she'd known since she was born.

"Myron. Carl. Please. I'm honored by your kindness. Truly, I am, but the boys and I are getting along great. Don't worry about us."

Myron's loose jowls jiggled insistently. "A woman needs a man to look after her."

That notion didn't set too well with Amy's independent spirit, but she didn't take offense.

"Leave Amy alone." A scowling Harry Peterson, owner-operator of Treasure Creek's General Store, slapped a pound of butter on the counter in front of Carl. The pot-bellied proprietor had been particularly grumpy lately. "Just because all those fancy women came flooding in here to find a man, doesn't mean every woman in town is interested in marrying you slobs."

"Ah, Harry," Carl said. "You're just mad 'cause Joleen's been flirting with Neville Weeks and he's flirting back."

Harry made a harrumphing noise and rattled a paper bag, the furrows in his brow deepening by the second. Amy had a feeling the old farmer had hit too close to home. Joleen Jones was a fluffy, overblown blonde who tried too hard, but she was as good as gold. She'd been hot after Harry since her arrival from Tennessee, but after so many rebuffs, the Southern belle had apparently given up. Amy felt sorry for the woman, though she had to wonder what Joleen saw in Harry in the first place.

"You gotta marry somebody, Miss Amy," Myron said as he scratched his wooly, gray beard. "Might as well be me. This town would dry up and die without you, and we want to help you out, now that Ben is gone."

The too familiar pang of loss sliced through the open wound Amy called a heart. Her husband, Ben, had died nearly a year ago, and though the agonizing grief had diminished, she didn't want to marry anyone.

Ben's last letter flashed through her head, but she instantly blocked it. He'd loved her and wanted the best for her, and Amy was not about to settle for less than a God kind of marriage such as they'd had. No matter what his letter had asked her to do.

She felt a responsibility to this historic little town, founded during the Yukon Gold Rush by her great-great-grandfather, Mack Tanner. She would fight with her last breath to keep it afloat, but that did not require marriage.

"Tell you what, Myron. I won't marry you, but I'll bake a batch of those cinnamon rolls you like. You, too, Carl."

Both men perked up.

Myron spoke for both of them when he said, "That's a better deal than getting hitched any day."

Amy agreed. With a smile and a wave, she gathered her bag of groceries and exited the store, nearly bumping into Reed Truscott, the local chief of police.

"Oops, excuse me," she said, sidestepping the tall, lean lawman.

He stepped in front of her, blocking the way. "How you doing, Amy?"

"Good. Yourself?"

He shifted in his boots, glanced across the quiet street and cleared his throat. The police chief obviously had something on his mind.

"Look, Amy, we need to talk. About this situation between us—"

She held up a hand, stop sign style. There was no *"situation,"* and if he asked her to marry him again—check that—if he *demanded* she marry him, she would stomp his toe. Of all the men who'd offered proposals, this was the one that bothered her most.

"Don't even think it, Reed. And do not say it. Whatever it is."

Whirling, she stalked off down the sidewalk. As she went, she heard him grumble, "Frustrating woman."

Well, it was frustrating to her, too. After Reed's first, arrogant, pushy proposal on the night of Ben's death, of all the inappropriate times, Amy had avoided any hint of personal conversation. She liked Reed Truscott, but she didn't pretend to understand his tight-lipped, overly macho attitude.

After picking up her two boys from the church preschool, Amy headed home, listening to their sweet chatter. As she pulled into the drive of her aging two-story clapboard and killed the SUV motor, an odd feeling came over her. She frowned at the blue house and then gazed around the yard, shrouded now in the hazy, dying light. Everything seemed all right. The red front door she'd painted herself beckoned cheerfully from its white, arched frame. Evergreens frosted with snow hugged the concrete steps swept clean this morning. And yet, her skin crawled in the oddest manner. Something didn't *feel* right, and after having a gun held to her head a few weeks ago, she'd learned to listen to that little voice inside. God was trying to tell her something.

Slowly, she exited the SUV and glanced around before getting Dexter and Sammy out of their car seats. She'd pull into the detached garage later. First, she had to check things out.

Four-year-old Dexter hopped down from the vehicle and bounded for the back door.

"Dexter, wait. Let Mama go first."

The dark-haired boy stopped and looked back at her, clearly puzzled by his mother's tone. Hoisting three-year-old Sammy and his ever-present stuffed dog onto one hip, she grabbed the groceries and her purse, balancing everything as she crossed the yard to enter through the back way, directly into the kitchen.

Stepping upon the single-stepped porch, her heart bumped. The back door stood ajar.

Had she failed to close it well this morning? The house was old and out of square. Some of the doors, including the back one, needed to be replaced and didn't fit properly—one more project that had ceased with Ben's death.

Easing Sammy to the ground, she scanned the yard and house again but saw nothing. Last night's snow revealed no footprints. Everything appeared normal except the open door.

Calling herself overcautious, she pushed the door wider and waited. After hearing or seeing nothing, she led the way into the kitchen.

"Oh, no!" The gasp tore from her throat.

Her house looked like a war had broken out and she'd been defeated.

Cabinet contents littered the floor. Jumbled drawers hung open like slack-jawed dogs. And the open refrigerator hummed incessantly, milk and juice spilling out in dripping puddles. Amy's hands fisted at her sides. Whoever did this had been searching for something. And she knew exactly what.

"Mom?" Dexter tugged on her jeans. Dark gray eyes, so like his father's, were as round as Frisbees. Above the tiny cleft in his chin, his bottom lip quivered. "Someone broke our stuff."

"It's okay, baby." Though of course, it was not okay. "Sammy, get away from that shattered glass."

The barely three-year-old, too small to comprehend the disaster, had dragged his stuffed pal, Puppy, straight into the broken, jumbled, sticky mess. She took his hand and tugged him back to her side. "Stay here by Mommy."

Grappling in her jeans pocket for the cell phone, Amy punched in a number. Her fingers shook.

On the second *brrr*, a strong, male voice barked, "Police department. What is your emergency?"

"Reed?"

"Amy?"

Regardless of his inopportune marriage proposal, she trusted Reed Truscott with her life.

"What's wrong?"

She drew a shaky breath, struggling to keep the fear out of her voice. "Someone broke into my house."

Reed hissed. She could practically see his lips drawn back and the tight expression on his face. "Are you okay?"

"We just walked in. This very minute." In spite of her determination to stay calm in front of the boys, Amy's voice began to shake along with her knees. "Everything's a wreck."

In the background, over the phone, she heard a drawer open and keys rattle. Chief Truscott was already moving. "Where are you?"

"In the kitchen." The flip phone quivered against her ear. "Whoever did this—"

Reed's sharp tone interrupted. "Have you been in any of the other rooms?"

Goose bumps rose on her arms. Her house was a two-story. "No."

She glanced down the hall leading from the kitchen to the side office. The normally comfortable space seemed ominously long and dark. Her gaze went to the small alcove off the dining room that housed the staircase to the second floor. Was that a squeak overhead?

Lord Jesus, protect us. Protect my boys.

Cradling the phone between her chin and shoulder, she grasped Dexter and Sammy by the shoulders.

"Take the boys and get out." Reed's usually calm tone tensed. "Do it now, Amy. Get out of the house."

He didn't have to tell her twice. Someone could still be inside.

"Amy? Do you hear me?"

"I'm going." If her knees would hold her up.

"I'll be there in five." The security of Reed's voice was lost as the line went dead.

Hurrying now, aware that her children could be in danger, Amy shuffled her sons out into the cold gray of a late November Alaska.

"Get in the car."

Ever alert to her surroundings, she opened the back door to the red SUV, hoisted Sammy and Dexter inside and quickly slammed the door. Car seats could wait.

More jittery than she wanted to be, she bolted around to the driver's side and hopped in. Her fingers trembled as she jabbed the key into the ignition, turned the switch and popped the locks. She leaned her head back against the seat and sighed but didn't close her eyes.

If someone was still in the house, she needed to know. If not for the boys, she would have searched the rooms herself and beaned the rats who'd invaded her safe and happy home.

But she had the boys to think about, and they came first—always.

As if he'd read her mind, Dexter leaned through the console. A tear trickled down his cheek. "I want Daddy."

Sammy heard the tremor in his big brother's voice. His

small head poked through the space, too. Tears streamed down his round, baby face. "I want Daddy, too. Where's Daddy?"

Both began to cry.

The words were a spear through Amy's heart. She wanted Ben, too. Even after nearly a year, she still expected him to walk in the door any moment, eyes dancing, face rosy from the outdoor work he loved. But Ben, her love, her best friend, her partner in Alaska's Treasures tour company, would never be here again to protect and comfort his sons. Or her.

The now-familiar heaviness pressed down on her chest. Life was not fair sometimes. She was strongly tempted to cry with her sons, but after Ben's death on the Wild Rapids Tour, she'd cried the Yukon River full of tears. Being strong for her boys and her floundering town were the things that mattered now. She had a job to do, people depending on her, and she would not fail them. Ben would have expected no less.

"Don't cry, Dex." She stroked her eldest's dark hair, so different from her own. "Come on. Crawl up here beside Mama while we wait for Chief Reed."

Dexter sniffed. "Is he coming? I mean, right now?"

"Any minute, baby."

Both her sons were more their father than her, which was fine with Amy, although looking into their faces was like looking at miniature versions of Ben. Dexter even bore Ben's chin cleft. The reminder was both pain and pleasure. She'd loved Ben James with everything in her. And he'd loved her the same way.

They'd been building a good life here in Treasure Creek, Alaska, where they had both grown up. The Alaska's Treasures tour company had been their dream, a dream that had cost Ben his life. But she never blamed the business or the lifestyle. Danger, like beauty, was part of life and work in rugged Alaska.

Without the revenue from the tour company and the

business it generated for the hotels, eateries and other enterprises, the little town of Treasure Creek could become another forgotten ghost town.

A siren ripped the cold, crisp air, and Amy found the sound as sweet as a Christmas carol. After another quick glance at the house, she turned to watch the rotating lights of Reed's four-wheel drive. His ever-present dog, Cy, sat in the passenger seat, mouth open in a smile.

Dexter stopped crying and moved to a side window. Sammy followed his big brother, dragging the stuffed puppy along at his side. Cy was a particular favorite of her two sons. The one-eyed malamute was usually more personable than his master.

Some of the tension left Amy's shoulders. Reed was here.

The tough, sinewy chief of police had been Ben's best friend. Regardless of that awkward, humiliating marriage proposal, Reed was a loyal friend and a great cop. Whoever had broken into her house had just made a fearsome enemy.

Reed Truscott slammed the vehicle into Park and bolted out the door before the truck stopped rocking. In more than a dozen years on the job, he'd never seen this much trouble in Treasure Creek.

"Mack Tanner and his treasure," he grumbled. People had been traipsing up on Chilkoot Trail for years, searching for the treasure Amy's great-great-grandfather had buried there during the Gold Rush of 1889. Why did the thing have to be found in his lifetime? And why did Amy have to be in the line of fire?

It was that crazy magazine interview Amy had done. That's what started all the trouble.

His boots crunched on last night's new snow as he stalked toward Amy's Jeep. Part of him expected Miss Iron Woman to still be inside the house. When he told her to get out, he'd intended for her to leave, to get completely away from the crime scene and any hint of danger. But Amy did things her way, so he was relieved to spot her and her little ones safely inside the red vehicle.

How was he supposed to take care of Ben's family when Amy was so uncooperative?

With her usual, vibrant energy, she hopped out of the car and came to meet him.

An invisible fist clutched his insides. Looking at Amy seemed to do that to him lately.

Stress, he supposed. Or responsibility. The problem had started after Ben insisted Reed take care of Amy and the boys if anything should happen to him. Reed had tried to laugh off the request, but when Ben pressed, he'd agreed. It was almost as if Ben knew he wouldn't be around to care for his loved ones. And Reed Truscott was a man of his word. He was honor-bound to look after Amy James. To his way of thinking, that honor was exactly why she should marry him.

But he probably shouldn't mention that to Amy today. She looked in no mood for another marriage proposal. He'd bungled the first time badly enough, though he was still trying to figure out where he went wrong.

Hands shoved into the pockets of her open parka, Amy strode toward him in jeans and a yellow-green sweater that turned her hair to copper fire. The cold, fading sunlight caught in the shoulder-length waves and shot sparks in every direction. She had glorious hair, the kind a man wanted to touch.

Reed's gut clenched again. He didn't like thinking of Ben's wife as pretty, but she was. Amy had been in his head and heart for a long time, first as a friend, but after Ben's death—well, things changed. And the feelings rolling around inside him were downright uncomfortable.

"You and the boys okay?" He barked the question, more worried about the town's main citizen than he wanted to show.

Amy nodded, pretending calm, but he'd heard the quiver in her voice on the phone. He was still angry about that. Any scuzzball who upset Amy was going to answer to him.

"Whoever broke in wasn't after us."

"This isn't the first time, Amy. Somebody will do anything to get their hands on that treasure of yours."

"I know." Her reply was quiet and reflective as she gazed off toward the mountains to the west. He knew she was remembering the day they'd finally found Mack Tanner's buried treasure chest. A pair of gun-toting thieves had found it at the same time.

He'd nearly had a heart attack when one of the thugs shoved a pistol against Amy's temple. If not for Tucker Lawson's help Amy could have been killed. That moment haunted his dreams.

Since this frenzy over buried treasure began he'd not had a moment of peace. Even though the heavy metal box was locked up in the safe in his office only he and Amy had that information.

The town's excitement wasn't helping, either. "Last rumor I heard down at the Lizbet's Diner estimates the contents of that box at over a million dollars."

Amy's eyes widened. "What? Reed, that's crazy. We don't even know what's in the box yet."

"Tell me about it. The price goes up every day." Grimly, he perched a hand on the butt of his service pistol. Until lately, he'd never worn it. Didn't need to. His adopted town was a peace-loving place, filled with good people. Mostly. "Men have killed for a lot less."

Amy had this crazy idea to wait until Christmas Eve, still four weeks away, to open the chest and present the treasure to the town. He understood in part because the town coffers were empty, and they needed money badly. The schools were in danger of consolidation, the library in danger of closing. Even his office budget was tighter than tree bark.

"You should open the treasure and be done with it," he said.

Amy took exception. "No! Treasure Creek has faced such difficult times these last couple of years. Thinking about this treasure and speculating about the good it will do for the town has lifted everyone's spirits. I will not allow low-life scums to rob us of the best Christmas possible."

Reed suppressed a sigh. He knew she'd say that. This was Amy, as tenacious as Alaskan winter and with a heart as big as the sun. All of Treasure Creek leaned on her, and she let them, encouraged them. Even though she was barely into her thirties, she carried a whole town on her small shoulders.

A man had to admire a woman like that.

But for the chief of police, Christmas couldn't come soon enough. Once the treasure chest was opened, maybe life would settle down and Amy would be safe again. Really safe.

He started up the drive. "I better have a look inside."

"I'll go with you."

"You and the kids stay out here."

"No way. If anyone was inside, they're probably long gone, but they also might be lurking in the bushes. I'll take my chances in the house with you."

Reed thought Amy might have just paid him a compliment. Though he'd rather she was somewhere safer, her logic made sense. An intruder could just as easily be outside as in. And Reed had the advantage of a loaded pistol.

They fell in step. As they passed Amy's vehicle, her two little boys tumbled out and followed.

"Chief Reed, someone broke our stuff."

Reed gazed down at the knee-high child. Dexter's little

head was tilted back, looking up with big gray eyes that trusted the police to do something. Police business Reed could handle, but kids were a puzzle. "Don't be scared."

It was a lame thing to say, but Dexter seemed okay with it. Like his mother, the child bowed his head, shoved his hands in his coat pockets and traipsed across the yard, ready to face whatever was inside the house. Three-year-old Sammy, though, clung to his mother's hand and stayed as close to her as possible. Reed couldn't help feeling sorry for the little guy.

They reached the back door and Reed thrust out an arm to stop them from entering. "Lock's jimmied. Was the door open when you arrived?"

Amy nodded. "Yes."

Incredulous, he stared down into eyes bluer than arctic waters. His gut did that weird clutching thing again. "And you went inside anyway?"

"This is Treasure Creek. I never used to lock my doors at all. You know how out of square this old house is. I thought maybe I'd forgotten to shut the door hard enough this morning before I went to the office."

A reasonable explanation, but he still didn't like the idea that she'd gone inside. If something happened to her—well, he felt guilty enough about the way Ben died without letting him down again.

"Let me go in first. You and the boys stay close until I check all the rooms."

Amy scooped Sammy onto her hip and held Dexter's hand, doing as Reed asked without comment. The break-in had shaken her more than she wanted to admit.

It had shaken him, too.

Together they made the rounds downstairs. Amy remained tight-lipped, but her pallor told how upset she was. They bumped in a doorway and it was all he could do to keep from pulling her close for a moment, to tell her everything would be all right, to erase the lines of worry around her beautiful eyes.

Reed slapped the impulse away. This was Ben's wife. She was his responsibility, not his woman.

"What a mess," he grumbled, mostly to break his troubling train of thought, but furious, too, at whoever had done this. "Upstairs next. Me first."

Whoever had been here was gone now. His gut instinct told him as much, but he was taking no chances.

As they started up, he reached out and took Sammy into his arms. The kid was barely three, but Amy wasn't as big as a house cat.

"I carry him all the time, Reed."

He just grunted and started climbing, his boots ringing hollow on the wooden steps. Lugging Sammy up the stairs was too much for her, whether she wanted to admit it or not. At the top, he returned the boy to his mother, needing to be alert and prepared in case of a nasty surprise.

"My room is here," she said, pointing to a green-paneled door. "I dread looking in there."

Reed bit down on his back teeth. He dreaded looking in there, too, but for more reasons than the break-in. Something about entering the bedroom that Amy and Ben had shared made him uncomfortable.

But he was a police officer. This was his job.

"Stay put. I'll look."

With the flat of his hand, he eased the door open and glanced inside. Anger bubbled up like a hot fountain. Ben had worked his tail off on this house. Reed knew, because he'd helped him. And now, like the rest of the house, the beige-and-blue bedroom was in shambles. Papers, books, clothes and toiletries were strewn everywhere. A lamp lay on the bed, the bulb broken and the shade crumpled. The room was as cold as the outside.

With a frown, he stepped inside. "Better come in here, Amy."

She did. "Oh, my."

The words were barely a breath, but they were filled with distress. Again, the need to hold and comfort assailed the chief of police.

Jaw tight, he pointed to the window. "Escape route. Your visitors were likely in the house when you arrived."

"I thought I heard something."

Frustration and worry and responsibility warred in his belly. This wasn't the first threat to Amy's safety. She was going to get hurt if he didn't do something and do it fast.

His inner voice demanded that he do the right thing—at least the right thing in his book—no matter how much personal turmoil it caused.

And so he did.

"That's it," he said. "You're moving in with me." He planted one hand on his hip and faced her, ready for the inevitable argument. "Today."

Chapter Two

Hair rose on the back of Amy's neck. Of all the arrogant, overreactive statements! She bit back a sharp retort while trying hard to see Reed's point. Ten seconds later she gave up. His point was ridiculous. Besides, the idea of moving in with Reed, for any reason, made her feel…funny.

"Don't be silly." She spun away and stalked out of the bedroom. Sammy and Dexter followed, little legs sprinting to keep up. They knew from experience that when Mommy moved, she moved fast.

She was already down the wooden staircase and making the turn toward the ransacked kitchen when Reed caught up with her. He grabbed her elbow. Amy stopped, not that she had much choice with fingers of steel and nearly two hundred pounds of muscle latched on to her.

"Come on, Amy, be reasonable. You have to."

Keeping her tone even, she said, "No, Reed. I don't. Now, kindly let go of my arm."

Reed glanced down at the place where he gripped and dropped her arm like a hot potato. He took half a step back, swallowed hard and looked about as comfortable as a grizzly in a tutu. If she wasn't so annoyed, Amy would have felt sorry for him.

"You're not safe here." Reed's words were ground out with all the gentle persuasion of a pencil sharpener. "You need protection."

"I can take care of myself." When the police chief looked as if he would argue, she held up one finger—and discovered the thing was still trembling. She yanked it down to her side. "The subject is closed. I am not leaving my home."

Especially to move in with Reed. The idea of being in the same house day after day with him was—well—strange. *Uncomfortable* for some reason—though they'd been friends forever. Maybe that was the point. Reed and Ben had been friends, and Ben's final letter to her niggled at the back of her mind constantly. He'd written the usual things at first—his love for her and the boys, his faith, the business—but then, as if he'd known he would never return, Ben had asked the unthinkable. If anything happened to him, he wanted her to find someone else. And he wanted her to do it before Christmas.

Now Christmas wasn't that far away. Neither was Reed Truscott.

Fact of the matter, he and the boys dogged her footsteps all the way into the kitchen. Reed stalked her like a grizzly—and growled like one, too. Her sons had the deer-in-the-headlights look as their eyes volleyed between her and the police chief. Neither said a word. Dexter, she noticed, edged up against Reed's leg. The police officer dropped a wide hand on her son's small shoulder. Emotion curled in Amy's belly, but was snuffed as quickly as a candle in gale force winds.

"I'm not suggesting anything illicit. My grandmother lives with me," Reed said, still grumbling and insistent. "It's not like we're in love or anything."

Amy fought down a blush. *Illicit? In love?* An uncomfortable flutter invaded her chest. Reed Truscott had to be the most confusing man on the planet.

To avoid his penetrating gaze, she turned a chair upright. Egg dripped off the seat cushion, the smell ripe. She curled her nose. Cleaning would take forever.

Keeping her voice even and cool, Amy said, "I think the world of your grandmother." Irene Crisp was a tough little sourdough who looked as if a good Chinook wind would blow her away. But looks were deceiving with Granny Crisp as well as with Amy. Reed should know that. "But I can take care of myself and my boys."

"You don't know what you're up against."

It was so like Reed to shoot out orders and expect them to be obeyed. Granted, he was a great cop and often right, though not in this case. "I appreciate your concern, Reed. Really, I do."

But she didn't want to hear another word about moving in with a man who could propose a loveless marriage and not understand why she turned it down.

With the subject closed—at least in her mind—she took Sammy's hand to stop him from going farther into the messy kitchen.

"Why don't you and Dexter go into the living room and watch TV while Mama cleans up?" she said to the upturned face. "Then I'll make some dinner, and everything will be back to normal."

Sammy wasn't buying it. He stuck a thumb in his mouth and shook his head. He hadn't sucked his thumb in a long time. Not since Ben's funeral. Dexter didn't move from his position next to Reed, but his gray eyes remained wide and worried.

Amy's heart pinched. She crouched down to their level. "Boys, we're okay. The bad guys are gone."

Sammy's wet thumb popped from his mouth. "Will they come back?"

Amy pressed her lips together and couldn't keep from looking at Reed. If he said one word—

"Whoever broke in wasn't kidding around, Amy. Look at this place." Reed made a wide arc with one arm, taking in the scattered belongings, opened drawers and spilled foods. "They *will* keep trying to find that treasure."

"Thanks a lot, officer," she said with a tinge of sarcasm. To the boys she said, "Tonight we'll make a tent in your room and all of us will sleep together. Just like one of Mama's wilderness tours. You can be the guides and I'll be the cheechako. Okay?"

Sammy nodded at the idea of Mama behaving like a greenhorn, but Dexter, wise and old at nearly five, was silent.

"I'm serious, Amy," Reed said. "You can't stay here. You have to let me help."

Help was one thing. Moving into his house was quite another. "No thief is going to run me and my babies out of the only home we've ever known."

She and Ben had spent blood, sweat and tears remodeling this old house that her ancestor, Mack Tanner, had built for his reluctant bride more than a hundred years ago. It was old and crotchety and drafty in the brutal months, but the place had character and was filled with love and wonderful memories.

Reed shifted heavily and it occurred to her, reluctantly, that he was as exhausted by the last few months as she was. Like her, Reed would not back down. His sense of duty was legendary. And it was that sense of duty that bothered Amy. She didn't want to be anyone's "duty."

"What if they come back?" he asked.

Her blood chilled at the thought. She rubbed her palms along the arms of her sweater.

"I'll manage," she said, with more bravado than she felt. She was single-handedly running a business, booking tour guides, dealing with love-hungry women, directing the annual church Christmas pageant and raising two little boys. She might be tired, but she could handle anything. "I'm not helpless, you know."

Dark eyes narrowed in Reed's rugged, weather-tanned face. "Never said you were."

She jammed a fist on one hip. "Same as."

Reed rolled his eyes heavenward. "You are the most exasperating…"

Amy couldn't help smiling. "Okay, tough man, why would your house be any safer than mine?"

"Granny is there. I'm there. Cy is there. We can protect you."

Amy scoffed. "Cy wouldn't hurt a hot biscuit." The malamute was gentle as a kitten.

"And—" he held up a finger as if to stop her argument "—my place sits off the road, up an incline that requires a four-wheel drive and a lot of patience to climb. It's backed by a mountain. No one can get to you there. Come on, Amy. Be reasonable."

Amy softened. Reed really was trying to do the right thing. He was misguided but well intentioned. "I'm not afraid to stay here." Not much anyway. "God has always taken care of me, and He won't let me down now."

Reed gave one grunt that let her know what he thought about that. His brown eyes glazed over and Amy suspected that he was thinking of Ben. Well, so was she. God had carried her through the nightmare of loss and the last year of struggling to make ends meet and to keep the town afloat. Without faith in God to sustain her, she would have given up.

Reed's gaze came back to hers. Jaw tight, he said, "Ben would expect me to take care of you."

Amy's hackles jumped up like barking dogs. Reed's twisted sense of loyalty to her dead husband was the final straw.

"I said *no,* Chief Truscott, and I meant it."

* * *

Reed was still stewing as he guided his Explorer back to the police station.

"She's going to get herself hurt, and then what?" If anything happened to Amy or her boys, he wasn't sure what he would do. A man could only live with so much guilt.

For one minute there, he'd been tempted to snatch her up, toss her over his shoulder like some barbarian, and drag her kicking and screaming to his place. Amy brought out the worst in him.

He shifted in the seat. Amy brought out something else in him, too.

"She's Ben's wife. End of story."

Only, Ben was gone.

The malamute in the passenger seat listened in silence, head cocked, his one good eye sympathetic. Reed reached across to ruffle the thick, dark fur. Cy was a lot easier to talk to than most humans, and a lot more dependable. A few years back, he'd given an eye to protect his owner, a fact that had earned him the right to sleep on the foot of Reed's bed. Reed Truscott put a lot of stock in loyalty. It was what had gotten him into this dilemma with Amy in the first place.

"Aw, Ben."

As much as he missed his good friend Ben James, he couldn't imagine how hard the man's death was on Amy. But Amy was a whirlwind, staying so busy with saving the world—or at least with saving Treasure Creek—that she didn't realize how much she needed a man's help. She'd give him an ulcer if he wasn't careful.

With a sigh, he ran a weary hand down his face. He hadn't slept well since this mess over the treasure had started. Actually, he hadn't slept well since Ben's death. Nightmares brought him back to that moment on the rapids when Ben threw himself into the icy water to rescue a capsized tourist and never returned. Some friend Reed Truscott proved to be.

With a groan, he tried to focus on something else. Thinking of his part in Ben's death drove him crazy. He'd been helpless then and he felt helpless now. But he still believed he should have done something.

He'd never told Amy about Ben's final moments but he replayed them often in his thoughts. Reed could almost feel the icy, snow-laden wind of that horrible January day, the slippery, snowpacked rocks beneath his feet, and the taste of fear in his mouth as he ran toward the river, sliding, falling, only to scramble to his feet and fall some more. He knew the capsized kayak was too far out and the rapids too wild and frigid, but he tried anyway. Long after Ben disappeared beneath the foam, Reed had searched by raft and on foot, and with every step, every stroke of the oar, he'd chanted his promise to care for Ben's family.

Though a search party eventually arrived, he'd been the one to find Ben's broken body hours later, far downstream—a sight that was burned into his memory with painful clarity. While he'd held his friend in his arms, knowing he and no one else must take the news to Amy, he sobbed his grim promise one last time.

He'd told her that night, and in the process, he proposed marriage. He thought it was the right thing to do. The thing Ben wanted. Amy hadn't agreed.

To make matters more insane, shortly thereafter Amy had been interviewed by *Now Woman* magazine. She talked about the handsome tour guides who worked for her, in an effort to promote the business, and now every love-starved female in the Lower 48 had converged upon the tiny Alaskan settlement noted for having more males than female residents.

"Maybe not every love-starved female," he conceded to his canine companion. "But too many."

Several had made a play for him, which just proved their desperation.

Still, a few of his buddies were now engaged or married because of that influx of females. They seemed happy about it, too. Not that he gave a frozen frog about love or marriage. He was too busy trying to keep the peace amongst all the ones who did.

Turning down Treasure Creek Lane, the town's main thoroughfare, he eased the Explorer over the snow-dusted street and into a parking spot outside the brightly painted facade of Alaska's Treasures tour company. Amy's business matched the other rustic-looking buildings—bright paint, clapboard and turn-of-the-century style.

Treasure Creek remained much as it had been in the Gold Rush Days. So much so that a man could close his eyes and imagine the rinky-tink of piano and the clip-clop of horse hooves that had filled the town a hundred years ago.

He climbed out of the SUV and sucked in the chilly smell of snow coming down out off the mountains. Treasure Creek enjoyed mild winters, comparatively speaking, and today's temperatures around freezing felt almost balmy. Black night would be upon them soon, and even now the streetlights sent a weak glow over the piles of shoveled snow. Dark or light, tired or rested, duty called the sheriff of Treasure Creek.

Amy employed a tight-knit group. The guides and office staff would want to know about the break-in.

"Come on, boy," he said to the waiting dog.

Cy leaped happily to the ground and shook out his fur, eager for exercise. His warm breath puffed gray around his muzzle as he hopped onto the curb. Reed moved more slowly, as tired today as he'd been as a teenager when he'd labored long hours on the freezing deck of a crab boat.

As far as his father, Wes Truscott, was concerned, his son was a dead weight who should be able to earn his keep. Reed had then, and he would now. Treasure Creek depended on him to keep its citizens safe. And that included Ben's widow.

Inside the small office of Alaska's Treasures tour company, he was greeted by the toasty, warm smell of fresh coffee and the friendly smile of Rachel Adams, Amy's receptionist. His belly growled, a reminder that his last meal had been somewhere around six this morning at Lizbet's Diner. Granny Crisp would have a hot meal in the microwave if he ever made it home.

"Amy's place was broken into," he said without fanfare.

Rachel's hand flew to her mouth. "Oh, no! Is she okay?"

"Fine." His answer was curt. "For now."

Gage Parker, one of the best search-and-rescue guides in the business, unwound himself from a chair where he'd been jotting notes on a yellow tablet. Next to him was his new wife, Karenna, and baby Matthew, Gage's nephew. The baby was trying to walk, holding on to the leather sofa as he toddled around.

Cy, who'd been waiting patiently next to Reed, ambled over and sniffed the little guy with interest. Matthew gurgled happily and patted the dog's head with an awkward baby pat. Gage and Karenna looked at each other with besotted smiles, as if no baby had ever done anything quite this adorable. The trio looked so right for each other, Reed got that heartburn feeling in his belly again. Love did weird things to people.

"What do you mean, for now?" Karenna asked, pulling Matthew into her arms.

"You know Amy. Too trusting for her own safety."

Gage snorted softly. "Typical."

The two men exchanged glances. Here, at least, was someone who understood Amy's propensity for being just a little too independent. He still didn't understand why she got all huffy when he'd asked her to move in with him and Granny.

The idea made perfect sense. Staying in that rickety old house of hers made exactly none.

By now, Rachel was out from behind the desk and passing the cubicles as she headed toward the back of the office where another door led into the meeting room. There, guides and Amy met to plan tours, hash out problems and otherwise run the business of taking tourists into the Alaskan wilderness. As Reed followed the blonde receptionist, the smell of coffee increased. Maybe he could snag a cup. Amy always offered. And if he was real lucky, there might be a donut or two back here with his name on them.

Rachel opened the door and hollered, "Hey, everyone, Amy's house was broken into."

The announcement was met with a sudden, stunned silence before chaos broke out. A chorus of concerned voices began asking questions Reed couldn't answer and expressing their general outrage that anyone would do such a thing—to Amy James, of all people. Amy, who was using everything she had to solve the town's financial crisis. Amy, who planned to donate her great-great-grandfather's treasure—worth an unknown fortune—to the town's coffers without a thought to herself. Amy, who was too stubborn to let him take care of her.

Reed took the final thought captive. He was still smarting from Amy's blunt, annoyed refusal. The truth hurt, but he got the point. Amy didn't want to be that close to him. But there was more than one way to keep his promise to protect Miss Independence. He knew Amy's employees, considered them friends. They had come to her assistance after Ben's death, and they'd stand by her now.

After a minute of noise, Reed raised one hand. "She'll need help cleaning up."

A tiny smile pulled at his lips. He'd feel a lot better knowing she had an army of friends on the lookout.

Before he left Amy's house, he'd found boot prints in the snow beneath her bedroom window, a fact he'd shared with Amy. Even that hadn't convinced her to move to his place. Instead, she'd flounced upstairs, come back down with a baseball bat and declared the puny thing an adequate weapon. By that point he'd given up.

He'd snapped some photos of the imprints, dusted the windowsill and other likely areas for fingerprints, but he didn't hold out a lot of hope of discovering who the perpetrator was anytime soon. He'd also personally locked every open window and relocked the doors. And he'd phoned the local handyman to fix the broken window in Amy's bedroom.

No matter what Amy said, she needed more than a baseball bat and her faith in God. If God was looking out for her best interests, why had the house been broken into in the first place? And why had Ben died on those rapids? Why hadn't Reed been able to get to him in time? He'd played the scene over in his head until he was nuts, and he still couldn't understand why he hadn't been able to save his best friend.

Guilt was a wicked companion.

Glass tinkled against glass as the willowy blonde and emminently elegant Penelope Lear swept a pile of shards onto a dustpan held by her sandy-haired fiancé, Tucker Lawson.

Penelope paused, one hand on Tucker's shoulder. The pair didn't have to say a word for everyone in the place to see how much in love they were. Though only recently engaged, Tucker and Penelope were a match made in heaven. And in the Alaskan wilderness.

"I don't understand why someone looking for the treasure would have to break your fine glassware," Penelope said to Amy, her tone totally disgusted.

Amy, busy sorting the ruined food from the salvageable, exchanged amused glances with Casey Donner, one of her guides and a dear friend. Both women were as practical as rain boots. Though a dear and gentle heart, Penelope was born a city girl, a wealthy socialite whose tastes ran to the finer things in life. Since coming to Treasure Creek, she'd toughened up considerably, following a wilderness trek that had almost cost her her life. Still, her expensive haircut and manicure were signs that Penelope would always enjoy the best. Amy's dollar-store tumblers probably weren't on Penelope's wedding registry.

"Don't worry about the dishes, Penelope. I'm just glad my boys are okay."

"Oh, Amy." Penelope's face paled. "I get a chill thinking about what might have happened if you had arrived home sooner."

So did Amy. Even now she dreaded the moment everyone would leave. No matter what she'd told her sons and Reed, she was badly shaken by the incident. The notion that some unknown enemy had handled her personal belongings inside the home she considered a sanctuary left her feeling violated and vulnerable.

Vulnerability was a luxury she couldn't afford.

"The important thing is she didn't." Nate McMann, one of her part-time, ultramasculine guides looked as out of place as Penelope as he crouched in front of the refrigerator with a scrubbing sponge. With his cowboy boots and Wrangler jeans, the rancher was more at home wrangling a five-hundred-pound steer than cleaning house.

"Aren't you scared to stay here by yourself?" Penelope asked, a tiny frown furrowing the perfect brow.

"I'll be fine," Amy said, but her thoughts returned to that moment of panic when she'd looked down the darkened hallway and wondered who might be lurking. A nervous knot spread from her belly to her shoulders.

"You could spend the night with me," Casey offered,

expressing concern. Wearing her usual cargo pants and unisex thermal shirt, Casey Donner was tomboy-tough, with a reputation for being as strong and capable as a man, even though, beneath the strength she was every bit a woman. As oilman Jake Rodgers had happily discovered.

"I appreciate the offer, Casey." Amy glanced toward the breakfast nook where Karenna Parker was playing with the boys and baby Matthew to keep them out of the way. "But I don't want my sons to think there's any reason to be afraid."

"But there *is* a reason, Amy," Penelope said with a graceful shiver. "You could get hurt."

Amy rubbed at the back of her neck. A headache was starting, and she was certain it was from tension. But running away from a problem never solved anything, and she was telling the truth when she said she didn't want her boys to know there was a reason to be afraid. Still, talking about the break-in upset her more than she wanted them to know.

"I'm glad all of you are here now. That's what matters. Let's just forget the other for a while, okay?"

Her friends exchanged glances and a silent agreement seemed to circle the room. No more talk of the break-in.

Nate dipped a pair of sponges into a bucket of soap suds and squeezed. Ketchup bloodied the water. "Business was slow anyway."

Amy forced her gaze from the red water and the reminder that she or the boys could have been hurt—that instead of ketchup, someone could have been cleaning away blood. "No calls this afternoon?"

Her voice sounded high and strained, even to her own ears. The last thing she or the town needed after the miniboom of that last few months was a dead week. Without tourists, the town could not survive.

Rachel looked up from the kitchen sink where she was washing anything anyone stuck in front of her. If the company's receptionist had closed the office, business must have been really slow.

"A few. Don't worry." Rachel waved a drippy skillet. "Snowmobile and ski season is upon us. We'll be wildly busy around Christmas and New Year's when the schoolkids are out on break."

"You're right, of course. The Lord has brought us this far. He won't let us fail now."

The pep talk was more for herself than anyone. Exhausted both physically and emotionally, she was running on fumes.

Nate pivoted on the toes of his boots. His green eyes rested on her, placid and sure. "Bethany's already booked a couple of December weddings. We're bound to attract a few tourists from those."

Amy's friend, Bethany Marlow, now Nate's fiancée, had returned to Treasure Creek a few months ago to establish a wedding planning business. Amy had once suffered doubts that such an enterprise was viable in the tiny town, but she'd been delightedly wrong. When Bethany moved back to Treasure Creek to set up her wedding shop, no one could have imagined how busy she would be. Although the now infamous magazine article had regenerated some unsavory interest in Amy's family's missing treasure, it had also proven a boon for the town.

The knot in her shoulders relaxed a little. Talking about weddings and business took the edge off.

"That's great news, Nate. Is the wedding party for anyone we know?" She glanced around pointedly at several faces glowing with love. Nate's was one of them.

"Not me and Bethany. At least not yet." He grinned, teeth flashing beneath his gorgeous green eyes. "She wants to make plans. Lots of plans. Gotta be perfect."

"Well, she *is* a wedding planner. Think of the publicity and the business the perfect wedding could bring. Not that either of you cares about that at your own wedding."

"You got that right." Nate was a tight-lipped rancher and part-time guide who naturally shied away from too much attention. Those who knew him knew the big wedding plans were a sure sign of how much he loved and wanted to please his bride-to-be.

"So if it's none of us, who *is* getting married?" Penelope asked as she dumped the dustpan into a large, plastic trashbag. Amy tried not to cringe at the clatter and clink of her broken belongings.

"A couple is coming up from Seattle to be married on skis, and Bethany's making all the arrangements, including accommodations for one hundred guests."

"A wedding on skis," Penelope mused. "Sounds…fun." Her expression said just the opposite.

Her fiancé, Tucker, laughed. "Does that mean you want to get married on skis, too?"

Penelope pointed a manicured nail at him. "You're cute, but you'll be even cuter in tails and a cummerbund."

"What? No skis?" Tucker teased. "No edgy Fifth Avenue goggles? No trendy pink-and-lime ski wear?"

"Only if you wear the pink," she said, eyes sparkling with mischief.

A couple of the rugged guides looked aghast at the conversation, but Tucker was an attorney from the city. Even though he'd spent months stranded in the Alaskan wilderness, he and Penelope weren't exactly the rugged type. But they were a perfect match. And he was the right groom for the formal wedding Penelope was planning—with Bethany's help, of course.

Amy laughed, more anxiety easing away as Tucker stalked a squealing Penelope into the darkened living room—a fitting place for two romantics to sneak a kiss.

When the pair returned a couple of minutes later starry-eyed and grinning, a twinge of envy caught Amy by surprise. She and Ben had once been like this, though the last few years, with the babies and the business, had been hectic and they'd had less time for each other.

"The B and Bs must be thrilled to have so many customers this time of year," she said.

Casey's short brown hair bounced against her face as she nodded. "I talked to Juanita this morning at Lizbet's Diner." Juanita Phillips owned and operated the Treasure Creek Hotel. "She said the hotel was booked solid through the New Year and already had Valentine's bookings, too. She's in shock."

"Good shock, if you ask me," Rachel said. "We need that kind of shock at the tour office."

A knock sounded at the door. Anxiety, momentarily at bay during the pleasant conversation, leaped into Amy's pulse. She jumped and spun, hand flying to her throat.

"Hey." Nate rose, giving her a worried look. He tossed the sponge into the bucket and came to stand next to her. "You okay?"

"Of course I am." Amy forced a smile. "The knock was unexpected. That's all." Burglars didn't knock. Did they?

Casey flipped on the back porch light and yanked the door open. The tomboy guide feared nothing. "Reed. Hi. Come in."

Hat in hand, the tall officer stepped inside. His gaze swept the room before landing on Amy. He frowned.

All her anxieties came rushing back and brought their friends along.

Chapter Three

Amy James was as slippery as a young salmon. No matter how hard he tried to keep an eye on her, Reed never quite felt in control of the situation. Even though he'd gone back to her house with the troubling news from Lizbet's Diner that a couple of strangers had been asking about the treasure, Amy had insisted on staying right where she was. She'd looked worried, nervous and shaken, but she'd thrust out that stubborn little chin and refused to even let him bring up the subject of moving to his place. As if he would have in front of half the town.

Short of camping on her doorstep in the frigid temperatures, all he could do was cruise past the cheerful blue dwelling every half hour after the unofficial cleanup committee gave up and went home. In a town as small as Treasure Creek, one deputy per shift was generally all the help a chief of police could afford, though during the busy seasons, Reed had a couple of part-time locals to call on. When exhaustion had overcome Reed, Deputy Ken Wallace had promised to keep an eye on Amy's place.

Eyes as gritty as sandpaper, he pulled his SUV into the garage attached to his ranch-style split-level. Dark was absolute at 2:00 a.m. in Alaska, but the dome light flared on when he opened the door and stepped out onto the concrete. Cy hopped down beside him and waited patiently at the locked entrance leading into the kitchen.

Though the garage was refrigerator-cold and ripe with the familiar smells of oil and grease, Reed paused on the single step to remove his boots. Granny Crisp was touchy about her clean floors. He took an old towel from a nail and carefully dried Cy's paws, too. No use getting Granny in a mood. He might own the house, but Granny was in charge of keeping things neat and tidy. For a little gnat of a woman, she could tear a strip off him with her black button eyes.

In his socks, he keyed the door and entered the kitchen, the only light glowing red from the microwave and stove clock. Cy's toenails clicked against Granny's polished linoleum. Reed reached for the light over the stove just as the overhead light flicked on. Temporarily blinded, he blinked rapidly until vision returned.

Granny Crisp stood in the doorway between the dining room and kitchen, a tiny twig of humanity. In gray thermal socks, a faded, red fleece robe that had seen too many washings, and sprouts of equally faded brown hair, she looked as harmless as a child. Reed knew better. The steel strength of her dark Russian ancestry ran through her veins.

Her gaze went first to his feet. He smiled inwardly. When it came to keeping a clean house, Granny was as predictable as the sunrise.

"Supper's in the oven," she said in her strong, blunt manner. Someone who didn't know her well might think her rude, but beneath the hard shell and sharp tongue was a loving granny who'd always been there for him.

"It's 2:00 a.m." With everything that went on today, Reed hadn't considered dinner, but right now all he wanted was a bed.

"I can tell time." She went to the microwave and pushed

three beeps worth of buttons. The whirring sound started. "Amy and her kids all right?"

Reed accepted his fate. He would have to eat before he could sleep. Granny's law. A working man needs to eat. He scraped a chair out and sat, leaning his forehead on the heel of his hand. "At the moment."

"You're worried."

"Wouldn't be up half the night if I wasn't."

"You don't worry about the rest of the town's residents this much."

Reed squinted at her. Granny knew him too well. "Don't start."

"Just saying." She slid a plate in front of him, yanked a chair away from the table and perched. Cy collapsed on the floor between them with a sigh, rested his snout on crossed feet and closed his eyes.

Reed filled a fork with a steaming cube of beef and brown gravy. "You can go back to sleep."

"Don't want to talk about it?"

"I'll clean up my mess."

She chuffed. "Not what I meant and you know it. Trouble's been brewing ever since word of old Mack Tanner's treasure got out again."

"Yeah."

"Why doesn't Amy give it up? Why not open the silly thing once and for all, so whoever wants it so badly will have to back off?"

This was Granny. Do the practical thing. Do it now. Get it over with.

"She has some notion that waiting until Christmas is good for the town. Says they need this for morale."

"Won't do anyone any good if a lot of people get hurt."

"No argument from me."

Granny was silent for a few minutes while Reed chewed

and swallowed, chewed and swallowed. Reed could practically see the wheels turning in her head.

"I think I see her point."

"You would."

"Don't sass." The admonition was mild and brought a grunt from Reed. "When times are hard, folks need hope. That treasure represents something bigger than the fortune it may hold."

If he hadn't been so tired, he would have rolled his eyes. "What it represents to me is trouble."

"In the form of a certain little redhead who doesn't know what's good for her?"

"I tried to get her to move out here with us."

Granny cocked her head, one eyebrow rising. "That a fact?"

"Temporarily." Reed's gaze slid away. He stabbed a piece of beef, not wanting to admit to Granny how distressed he was over Amy's refusal.

"Did you ever consider that a woman might want something more permanent in her life?"

A knot formed in his gut, a familiar phenomenon of late, with the issue of Amy and her boys ever on his mind. Granny didn't know about the ill-fated proposal. Make that *proposals*. What would she say if she did?

"She had Ben," he mumbled, and then shoved his mouth full.

"Had."

As if he needed another reminder that Ben was past tense and Amy James was unattached.

Two days after the break-in, Amy was starting to feel comfortable in her own home again. She regretted the loss of the lamp she and Ben had bought on their first anniversary, and she was furious that her photo albums had been ripped, but overall, she, Sammy and Dexter were okay.

Now, if the chief of police would find someone else to worry about, she'd be perfect.

Okay, maybe not perfect, but surviving.

She plopped down on the foot of Dexter's bed to pull on clean socks. Since the break-in, she'd slept in with the boys. Even though she claimed the move was for them, she felt safer in their room than hers. The thought of an unknown man—if it was a man—rifling through her underwear drawer gave her the creeps.

"Mama?" Dexter jumped onto the bed next to her.

"What, baby?" Tonight was practice at the church for the Christmas pageant. Time to break out her collection of crazy Christmas socks and to put away her Thanksgiving turkey tubes.

"Do you know what the teacher asked us today?"

"What?" She paused in sliding on a pair of lighted Rudolph knee-highs to smile down at her handsome son. Dexter and Sammy attended the preschool at the church and were forever asking, "Do you know what?"

"Teacher asked what we wanted to be when we grow up. Know what I said?"

"A cliff diver?" Last year, he'd seen a TV program on the subject and declared this his life's ambition.

"Nope. A policeman. Like Chief Reed."

Oh. "You'll make a fine police officer. Now, get your shoes on. We're leaving soon."

Dexter somersaulted from the bed and landed loudly and in a sprawl beside his shoes. "I might be a gymnast, too."

Amy held back a smile. "Very useful in police work."

Little Sammy, playing happily on the rug with Hot Wheels, looked up. "When I gwow up, know what I'm gonna be?"

"What?"

His baby face full of innocent sincerity, he said, "A pink dolphin."

Sputtering with laughter and filled with joy, Amy swooped down upon her two sons for a noisy wrestling match on the rug. No matter how stressful life became, Dexter and Sammy made every day worthwhile.

"Chief Truscott, welcome."

Reed nodded politely as he ran a cautious gaze around the chaotic scene inside the sanctuary of Treasure Creek Christian Church. He preferred calm and controlled, though lately he'd settle for controlled. Calm hadn't reigned in Treasure Creek in months. He spoke before he thought. "Noisy."

Jenny Michaels, the pastor's friendly wife, chuckled. "If you think this is noise, stop by the day care sometime."

Reed allowed a half smile. Mrs. Michaels, in her mid-forties, with short, coifed blond hair, a moderate overbite, and a pair of reading glasses hanging around her neck, was known in town as a kind, gentle woman with a passion for children's ministry. She also ran the church's day-care center and preschool. Amy's kids attended the center. "Amy here yet?"

If the reverend's wife thought it odd that he asked after Amy James, she didn't react. Instead, she glanced at her watch. "Running late. Must have gotten delayed at the office."

A frisson of alarm skittered along Reed's nerve endings. It was past seven and dark as pitch outside. Amy had no business being out there alone. When he'd asked earlier in the day, she'd told him she would be here tonight, directing the Christmas pageant just as she was every Tuesday night at seven. She'd also added the oft-repeated invitation for him to join the festivities. So here he was, though not to join the festivities, but to keep an eye on a certain redhead who didn't comprehend the threat to her safety.

"She should be here by now." He reached for his cell phone and began stabbing numbers.

Mrs. Michaels lightly touched his arm. "There she is."

Sure enough, Amy, flanked by her sons, blew through the door like a swift, fresh breeze. Reed's chest clutched. He jammed his cell phone into his pocket and stalked toward her. "Are you all right?"

Amy ground to a halt in the entry between the foyer and the sanctuary. "Reed! What a surprise. I'm glad you could make it."

From the expression in her amused blue eyes, Amy suspected his presence at the church was not for spiritual reasons. She was right. He was here to keep an eye on her. And she wasn't cooperating.

Before he could find out why she was late, someone called her name. He glanced up to see Penelope Lear bending over a large cardboard box. "Amy, come look at the shepherds' costumes Bethany made. They're so cute."

"Be right there."

Before she could move, Renee Haversham came rushing toward her, trailing an electrical cord. "Amy, one of the microphones shorted out. What are we going to do?"

While she was talking to Renee, Joleen Jones appeared. Joleen was one of the newcomers, her overdone makeup and big hair a dead giveaway that Alaska was not her native land. She was a silly thing, jumping on every man in sight. Reed had an urge to run every time they met.

"Amy, Greg has the flu. Can I have his solo part? I've been practicing. Listen. 'Fear not, for behold,'" Joleen's high-pitched, annoying voice rose as she dramatically threw one arm high into the air. "'I bring you good tidings of great joy, which shall be to all people.'"

"Wonderful, Joleen. Really. But let's just pray that Greg will recover by then. We have more than three weeks."

Joleen looked a little crestfallen, but didn't argue.

In a matter of seconds, Amy was surrounded by people, all asking questions or announcing problems for her to solve.

"Amy, who's doing the programs?"

"Check with Nadine on those. She agreed to type them up."

"I asked her already. She has conjunctivitis. Can't use the computer."

"I'll take care of them. Don't worry."

"Amy, the silver glitter is on back order."

"I'll talk to Harry. Maybe he can get it somewhere else."

Reed watched in wonder as Amy fielded each concern with equal aplomb, all the while working her way down the aisle, away from him and toward the front, where yet another army of pageant participants waited.

He'd thought she needed protection from the treasure thieves, but now he wondered if she couldn't use a bodyguard here at church. Even with her antlike energy, the woman had to get tired.

A small, sturdy body slammed into his lower leg. Small arms twined around his kneecap. He glanced down into the serious gray eyes of Amy's older son.

"Chief Reed, are you going to be in the pageant? Mama said you'd make a great Joseph."

Why would she say a weird thing like that? The only time he'd been in a Christmas program, he'd been ten years old and the director had cast him as an angel, complete with halo. The only reason he'd done it was the bag of candy waiting when the program ended. Well, candy and Granny Crisp. That was the last time he could remember attending church. After that, his father dragged him off to the Aleutians and a rough fisherman's way of life. Granny Crisp said he needed to get his spiritual house in order, but—well, churches made him uncomfortable. Like now, when a small boy with Ben's cleft chin was clinging to his leg like a barnacle. He never knew what to say to kids, so he simply rested one hand on the boy's hair. Had his own hair, now coarse and springy, ever been that fine?

"Chief Reed?"

"What?" Reed said absently as he scanned the room for Amy. The tiny redhead stood on the dais, arms gesturing, trying to direct the group into their places. She looked like a red ant trying to control a herd of sheep. A really pretty red ant.

"Where's Cy?"

"In the truck."

"Why?"

Reed glanced down. "His feet are wet."

"Yours, too," the boy said, looking pointedly at Reed's glistening boots.

Strike one. Try again. "No dogs in church."

Dexter's gray eyes blinked, then widened, his voice aghast. "Doesn't Jesus like dogs?"

"Sure He does." *I guess. I mean, how would I know?*

"Then why won't He let Cy come in the church?"

Reed cast around for an answer that would satisfy the inquisitive child and keep himself out of hot water with Amy. If he told Dexter that Jesus didn't like dogs, she'd skin him alive. Besides, he knew very little about Jesus's likes and dislikes. Other than sin. He knew Jesus was nice to people and didn't approve of sin. Dexter adored both Cy *and* Jesus. No use causing conflict. "Loud music hurts his ears."

"Jesus's ears?"

Holding back a grin, Reed said, "Cy's. A dog's ears are very sensitive."

"Oh. Can I pet Cy after practice?"

"Sure. Anytime."

Apparently satisfied, Dexter loosened his grip on Reed's

thigh and meandered away toward his younger brother, who'd taken up with Casey Donner. Casey, ever the rough-and-tumble tomboy, had scooped up the smallest James child and was toting him around on her back. Reed could rest easy as long as they were with Casey. She'd wrestle a charging moose for one of those boys.

"Come on up front and sit down, Chief Truscott." Mrs. Michaels was back, smiling her serene, toothy smile. "The choir will get started in a minute. Amy's put together a lovely program this year."

Feeling as out of place as a walrus, Reed nodded politely and moved toward the front. He could keep a better eye on Amy this way. Instead of slipping into one of the pews, he leaned against the wall and crossed his arms.

Ethan Eckles, a talented musician who taught school and worked as a part-time guide for Amy, struck a chord on the piano, and the noise in the room ceased.

The quiet was short-lived.

Chapter Four

Amy was acutely aware of Reed Truscott staring at her from across the room. She could practically feel his dark eyes lasering through the back of her Christmas-green cable knit. He didn't fool her one bit. He'd never so much as darkened the doors of this church, and now, there he was, looking as dangerous and rugged as the Chilkoot, filling up the room with his protective presence. When was he going to get the message that she could take care of herself? She disliked being someone's responsibility—especially his.

Her conscience pinched. *Sorry, Lord,* she thought. *I'm glad he's here, no matter the reason. Forgive me for being so prickly.*

It was true. Being around Reed disturbed her. Regardless of her protestations to the contrary, she had the insane urge to be close to him. All that terse, macho protectiveness was beginning to feel…nice.

But if she let him know, he'd start up with his ridiculous, condescending proposal again, reminding her that he didn't love her, but that he'd promised Ben.

"Mommy?" Sammy's little voice broke through her thoughts. He and the other children not in the program were supposed to be in the children's room, playing games. "Can I stay up here by you?"

Amy sighed. Ever since the break-in, Sammy had not wanted to be out of her sight. He snuggled tight to her at night and clung during the day. He was sucking his thumb too much again, as well.

"Chief Reed is here," she said, knowing instinctively that this would reassure him.

Her son's face brightened. "He is? Where?"

Aware that Reed was watching with his sharp, hawk eyes, she slowly pivoted, turning Sammy with her. She pointed. "Over there. By the wall." *Staring a hole through my back.*

"Can I go stand by him?"

She wanted to be the one to give her son confidence, but so far she'd failed. "You can stay up here with me. We're safe, Sammy. The chief is here and so am I."

She didn't like using Reed this way, but she'd do whatever helped her son get over the recent trauma. And she really was glad to see Reed in church, even if he wasn't here for the right reasons. Being here at all was a start. She and Ben had invited him often, had witnessed their faith to him, and while he was never outright rude, Reed remained quietly resistant, always using his job as an excuse. For once, his job had brought him to God's house.

Dragging the black, flop-eared, stuffed Puppy that had seen too many washings, Sammy trudged to the front pew and curled up, his small, booted feet poking off the edge. Maybe he'd go to sleep.

Satisfied, Amy turned back to the mingling, chattering group assembling in the choir area. Ethan Eckles shuffled pages of sheet music on the piano. Ethan, an elementary school teacher, also worked as a part-time tour guide with her company. Some folks were surprised by the rugged Alaskan's musical prowess, but Amy wasn't. There was an artistic side to the man she'd come to know, behind the quiet, brown eyes and chiseled jaw.

"Ethan, are you ready to get started with choir practice?" As director of the Christmas pageant, Amy organized every single detail, but Ethan directed the choir and played the piano.

"Delilah's not here yet. Neither is Harry."

Delilah Carrington—though she couldn't carry a tune in a fishing boat—was normally the first one to arrive and the last one to leave. Since giving her heart to the Lord a few weeks ago, Delilah was an enthusiastic member of the pageant, singing, decorating and even buying props with her own money. For her to be late was odd. Harry Peterson, on the other hand, was never on time. The powerful bass singer would eventually jog in, grumbling about something or someone holding him up at the General Store.

Lately, he was even grumpier, and Amy suspected Joleen Jones was the reason, although Harry had done his best to drive away the overeager Southern belle. Amy kept hoping both of them would get a double dose of the Christmas spirit.

"I hope everything is okay," Amy said. "But we need all the practice we can get to pull this off. We'll have to start without them."

Joleen, bleached platinum hair fluffed like cotton candy and vermillion mouth talking a mile a minute, had already taken her place next to Neville Weeks in the choir. At the mention of Harry's name, she'd gone silent, one beringed hand pressed against her throat. Amy felt sorry for the woman. Why she adored Harry Peterson was a mystery, but she did. After she'd chased—and alienated—nearly every man in town, the grumpy, pot-bellied proprietor of the town's general store had won her heart. And broken it.

Ethan took over, quietly and patiently instructing the choir as if they were a bunch of fidgety elementary students, and the off-key, endearing sounds of Christmas began. Amy had maneuvered the microphones so that the best voices were near the speakers and the worst were in the back, staggering them according to height and voice.

She made a mental note to check with Pastor Michaels about the choir robes. The old burgundy robes would do fine, if the church could come up with the money to have them cleaned and pressed and to replace the worn, white stoles with new forest-green ones.

Satisfied that Ethan had the music under control, she headed for the stairs up to the balcony, where the teenagers and several of the men, led by Gage Parker, were setting up lighting. She glanced back to see Sammy trailing her, dragging Puppy.

Inadvertently, her gaze went to Reed. Sure enough, he was watching. A warm flush slid up the back her neck. Reed pushed off the wall as if to follow her, too. She held up an index finger to stop him. She would not be stalked by the town's police officer, not even for her own good—*especially* for her own good.

Reed's jaw tightened as he squinted her way. After a silent battle of wills, his chest rose and fell in a huff. He recrossed his arms and leaned back into his place on the wall, though his eyes remained fixed on hers.

Amy hovered on the stairs, holding Sammy's hand while the sound of "It Came Upon a Midnight Clear" swelled around her, the familiar old hymn filling the church and her spirit. Lighted Christmas wreaths ringed the sanctuary walls. One was positioned directly above Reed and set his dark skin aglow. His brown-black hair was mussed from the wind and the ends glistened damply. He'd unsnapped his dark blue service jacket and it hung open to reveal the lean officer's shirt, complete with patches and badge and unidentifiable service pins. Reed Truscott was a handsome man in a rugged kind of way.

Amy's stomach fluttered. She tried to blame the reaction on the bulge of what could only be a gun at Reed's side. A weapon in church didn't seem right.

One thing for sure, she needn't worry about the thieves if he was around. Reed would take care of her and the rest of Treasure Creek. It was, as he constantly reminded her, his duty.

"Amy?"

Relieved at the distraction, Amy turned toward the female voice coming from above.

A troubled face, surrounded by bouncy red ringlets, looked down at her from the top of the stairs.

"Delilah! I didn't know you were here. Why aren't you rehearsing with the choir?"

In Ugg boots, snug jeans and a sheepskin vest, Delilah was fashion personified, though not nearly as high fashion as she'd once been. She and the other women who'd come to Treasure Creek were quickly learning that high fashion and Alaskan winters didn't jive all that well.

The petite young woman shrugged. "I don't really feel like singing tonight."

Though she usually put on a happy face, Delilah was a new Christian, and she still struggled with feelings of self-worth. Though they were close in age and very similar in size and looks, Amy felt eons older than Delilah, and had taken it upon herself to mentor and encourage her new friend. She trotted up the stairs. "Want to talk about it?"

Delilah gazed around at the chaos of people discussing, stringing lights and speakers, and setting up props, all of them clamoring for Amy's input. "Do you have time?"

Amy made a face. "We'll make time. Come on. Let's grab a cup of hot chocolate." To the working masses, she called, "Be back in a bit. You guys know what to do."

"Sure, Amy," someone hollered. "We've got you covered."

The notion warmed her heart. This little town pulled together. They *did* have her covered.

She and Delilah maneuvered the stairs again, this time heading down. As they reached the side door and were exiting the sanctuary, Amy glanced back to see Nate talking to Reed. Good. He didn't notice her. It would be embarrassing to have the town police chief follow her around the church like a bodyguard.

Concerned about what could be troubling Delilah, she put Reed out of her mind and headed through the exit and down the long hallway toward the fellowship hall, which did double duty as an all-purpose room. Sammy and his faithful Puppy trailed along, holding her hand. She stopped at the children's church and urged him to go inside. The noise and activity of half a dozen playing, laughing children drew him in, and before she closed the door, Amy saw the nursery worker lift Sammy onto her lap and open a book. Sammy loved stories. He would be okay for a while.

Once inside the fellowship hall, Amy went to the counter that separated the kitchen from the dining area. "There's hot cider and cocoa in packages. Coffee in the pot."

"Coffee's okay with me." Delilah sounded glum, as though nothing mattered, especially coffee.

Comfortable in her childhood church, Amy took two disposable cups and handed one to her friend. Needing the buzz of energy from a good cup of chocolate and sugar, she said, "Cocoa for me."

The big room was amazingly empty, though Amy knew it would not remain that way long. Folks would meander in for refreshments soon, and many of the props were being created here. Even now, the smell of paint hung in the air and a cardboard camel, festooned with a braided turquoise halter, leaned against one wall. Glittered stars were spread across another newspaper-covered table. And a pile of tools and lumber littered one corner.

Silently, the women made their drinks and then settled at one of the empty folding tables. Amy's shoulders relaxed in the familiar, homey setting. She had enjoyed many dinners and celebrations in this room, and the place never failed to evoke happy memories. Her wedding reception had been held here, and both her babies had been welcomed with showers in this very place. She was a blessed woman in so many ways.

She looked across the table at Delilah, realizing that her friend had no such happy memories to sustain her through hard times. From their brief talks, she'd learned that Delilah had grown up in California, the child of low-budget actors whose focus had been on making it big and being seen, rather than making memories with their child. No wonder Delilah sometimes came on too strong.

Amy sipped at her cocoa, then wrapped both hands around the warm cup and waited.

Delilah stirred sweetener into her coffee, then lay the spoon aside. The metal clinked softly against the Formica tabletop. "You're going to think I'm crazy."

"Between the treasure, the engagements, the weddings and now Christmas, we're all a little crazy. Join the crowd."

This at least got a smile out of the depressed Delilah.

"Well, I'm crazier than most." She sipped her coffee and Amy waited, knowing the conversation would come. "It's the engagements that have me thinking. Everyone is finding Mr. Right, getting engaged or married. Sometimes I feel like such a fool. I came here dreaming of finding the perfect man and now…"

Amy smiled against her cup. Delilah and plenty of others thought Treasure Creek, Alaska, was the answer to their romance problems. At the same time, she felt sorry for Delilah and the others who were lured by the promise of handsome men under their Christmas trees.

"Sometimes I wish I'd never given that magazine interview," Amy admitted.

Delilah looked stricken. "But then we'd never have met. And I'd never have found Christ."

Instantly repentant, Amy reached over and patted Delilah's small hand. "I didn't mean that. A lot of good has come out of that article." If not for the influx of tourists, the town would be well on its way to becoming another of Alaska's ghost towns. "I was just thinking how disappointed you and a few others have been. The magazine led you to believe something that wasn't true."

"Oh, but it is true. There are plenty of rugged, handsome, manly men in Treasure Creek."

And Delilah had chased them all. That was the problem. She had come on so strong that most of the men had run backward to escape her obvious man-hunting. Delilah was pretty and outgoing and charming in her own way, but she was only just now learning that being obnoxious and overbearing—even in a fur coat, fancy clothes and expensive Ugg boots—was not attractive.

"I thought you were interested in Corey Martelli."

Delilah lifted one shoulder. "Not really. Not anymore. He's cute and all, but he's not my type."

"Who is your type?"

"You're going to think I'm crazy."

Half of Treasure Creek already did. Delilah had started planning a wedding—without a groom—the moment she'd hit town. Amy smiled. "You already said that. So tell me."

"Promise not to laugh."

Amy crossed her heart. "Promise."

"Ronald Pfifer."

With a frown, Amy said, "I don't think I know him."

And she knew practically everyone in and around Treasure Creek.

"You wouldn't. He's from back home in L.A."

"Ah, an old flame."

"More like an old friend. We grew up together—Ronald on one side of the street and me on the other. He was always there. My nerdy, redheaded best friend with thick glasses and a big nose. I cried on his shoulder every time a boyfriend dumped me."

"He sounds like a very nice man."

"Oh, he is. He's so sweet." Delilah's eyes took on a dreamy quality. "We even had this pact that if we weren't married by the time we were thirty we'd marry each other."

"Oh." Delilah could be silly, but she was a romantic who longed for love, and Amy couldn't imagine her settling for someone just because she'd reached a certain age.

"I know how shallow that sounds. I didn't before, but now I do."

Amy smiled. God was making some changes in Delilah Carrington.

"When I told Ronald I was coming here," Delilah went on, "he shocked me to the soles of my stilettos."

"How?"

"I foolishly told him I was coming to Alaska to find my perfect soul mate. Ronald became terribly upset, more upset than I'd ever seen, and called off our pact. We haven't spoken since. At first, I didn't understand his behavior, but—"

Amy saw the problem. "He was in love with you. Really in love. And you thought of him as only a friend. A backup groom."

"Exactly. He loved me. And I was too callous and selfish to realize how much I was hurting him. Oh, Amy, how could I have done that? Ronald may not be a muscled hunk on the outside, but he's got more muscle in his brain than anyone I've ever known. He taught me to play chess and how to balance my checkbook. He even invested my money and taught me how to build a fail-safe portfolio. Most of all, he listened and cared about me, even when I was so silly and shallow, thinking of nothing but parties and clothes and boyfriends. Ronald is such a good man, and he has the prettiest brown, puppy dog eyes. But I treated him abominably. There is no way he could forgive me."

"Do you love him? Or just feel badly for what you did?"

"I love him, Amy. And it took coming here to open my eyes."

The poor girl looked so miserable, Amy's heart hurt for her. "Then you have to talk to him. At the very least, Ronald deserves an apology."

"I've tried. That's why I'm depressed. Two days ago I emailed him, but he never replied."

"What did you say?"

"I told him about becoming a Christian, and that I was sorry if I'd hurt him and that I'd really, really love to discuss something important with him."

"And no answer?"

"Not a word."

"Maybe he hasn't checked his email."

Delilah rolled her green, thick-lashed eyes. "Ronald Pfifer is a computer nerd. He lives with an iPhone in his hand."

Amy's lips curved. "I see your point."

"So I guess that's that. I've missed my chance with the one man who might be the real Mr. Right. All because I was too silly to see what was right under my nose."

"I'm sorry, Delilah. I really am." Although she was not the best person to give advice to the lovelorn, Amy understood disappointment and loss.

At that moment, three men entered the room: Pastor Ed, Dr. Alex Havens, the town's pediatrician, and Reed Truscott. A buzz of energy shot into Amy's bloodstream, and she couldn't decide if the cause was cocoa or Reed. And if it was Reed, why?

"Nice of you to help, Chief," Pastor Ed was saying. "We can always use a man who's handy with a hammer."

Oh. He wasn't following her. He was here to help the men. Shouldn't she be glad about that?

"Which leaves me out," joked Dr. Havens. "The only hammer I use tests the reflexes. But I wield a mean can of paint."

The friendly doctor glanced their way and smiled. Avoiding Reed's gaze, Amy lifted her empty cocoa cup to Alex. In the past, Delilah would have jumped up and simpered all over the good-looking physician, as well as Reed. The fact that she didn't only proved how far she'd come.

Lord, Amy thought, *open Ronald Pfifer's heart—and his email.*

Delilah took a final drink of her well-cooled coffee and then pushed back from the table. "Do you think it would be useless if I sent Ronald a Christmas card? I don't want to appear pushy."

Amy nearly choked on her hot chocolate. Delilah worried about being pushy? After a quick swallow, she said, "I think a card would be exactly the right reminder. And you never know, a little prayer for Ronald's forgiveness might help, too."

Delilah reached out and squeezed Amy's arm. "Thanks for making me feel better. Maybe I can sing after all."

As Delilah headed back out to the choir, a dozen other people entered the room. Some headed straight for the refreshments. Others went to the tables to work on props. Amy couldn't keep from glancing toward Reed. He seemed in deep conversation with Pastor Ed, as they sorted through the stack of lumber and selected tools. He didn't appear to notice her at all.

Amy rotated her head, aware of the kinks tightening her neck muscles. She hadn't realized how tired she was until she'd sat down for a few minutes. Since her arrival an hour ago, she'd been too busy to think. And there was still plenty left to do.

Renee Haversham stuck her head around the door and called, "Amy? Everyone is here now. We're ready to rehearse the acting parts whenever you are."

She reached for the program script she'd placed on the chair next to hers. "On my way."

Reed swung the hammer and drove a nail deep into the wood. With one hand holding the manger leg in place and the hammer drawn back, he spotted Amy disappearing out the door.

Frowning, he thought about following. The woman flitted around as much as a red wasp on caffeine.

"Quit worrying, Chief." Pastor Michaels clapped a hand on his shoulder. "Whoever broke into her house won't bother coming to church."

Was he that obvious?

With a grunt and a concerted effort to change the subject, he motioned toward the wood glue. "I'll need that in a minute."

The crude manger was shaping up fast. Not that he considered a cattle trough much of a challenge.

"You sure know your way around a piece of wood," Jake Rodgers said. His fiancée, Casey Donner, stood next to him, sorting through the remaining lumber. Reed thought the oilman and the tomboy guide were an odd couple, but from the looks they exchanged with sickening regularity, they were crazy about each other.

"Thanks."

"We could have used you last week on the stable frame."

"You saying my carpentry wasn't good enough?" This remark from Gage Parker came with a grin. There wasn't much the rugged tour guide couldn't handle, including a piece of wood.

"Nope," Jake answered. "Just saying I haven't seen a man drive a nail in one swing in a long time."

Working on a crab boat all those years had made Reed's hands and arms as strong as anvils. Since coming to Treasure Creek, he'd kept busy working on his own place, as well as helping Ben. Light carpentry like this was no big deal. Still, it felt good to feel useful, instead of being propped against a wall where he stuck out like a sore thumb. Helping had taken away the uncomfortable fish-out-of-water feeling. The faint sound of Christmas carols drifting in from the choir was nice, too.

Maybe hanging out at church wasn't so bad after all. Just when his shoulders were starting to relax, a high-pitched scream ripped the air. "Help! Somebody. Hurry!"

The voice was female.

Reed's adrenaline spurted. He dropped the hammer and ran. As he bounded down the hall, radio and keys and weapon jostling, all he could think of was Amy and her sons. If some creep had busted into church, of all places, and accosted Amy, the dirtbag was about to be very sorry.

Everyone else in the church was moving toward the cry for help as well, and Reed had to push through the sea of bodies to enter the sanctuary. Someone pointed upward and he skidded to a stop. Above them, in the balcony, Penelope Lear struggled with a ten-foot tall, decorated Christmas tree that had become unbalanced and canted dangerously to the right. Shiny red balls and flashing lights clanked against one another. Amy and the doctor's wife, Maryanne, were rushing to the rescue but hadn't yet reached the falling tree.

"It's coming down," someone said. Tension thickened in the room.

Though immeasurably relieved that the distraction was not criminal, but still full of adrenaline that needed release, Reed bounded up the stairs two at a time. Alex Havens and Tucker Lawson, he noticed, were right behind him. Understandable. Their women were up there.

Reed reached the women first, and for reasons he refused to consider, slid in next to Amy. Adding his long arms, Reed reached in to the tree trunk and pushed. His nose twitched at the weird, plastic scent. Whatever happened to real trees?

Amy's slender, sweater-clad arm brushed his as they righted the tree together. Unlike the fake pine, Amy smelled really nice. Like Christmas cookies and cocoa.

His own thoughts annoyed him. Next, he'd be thinking about how pretty she was again. And that wouldn't do. His job was to protect her, not to notice her pretty hair and soft skin and bright blue eyes.

Reed intentionally gripped a wad of artificial pine needles in his palm and squeezed, figuring he deserved the pain.

When Amy grinned up at him, Reed, still fighting his emotions, blurted, "You're determined to get hurt, aren't you?"

The light in her eyes went out, replaced by an arctic frost. She looked past him to the other men. "Will you guys stabilize this and check the other one, too?"

Then she turned and left the balcony.

Reed wanted to kick himself. Why did he always say the wrong thing?

"Have you finally put out all the fires?"

At the quiet, familiar voice of Reed Truscott, Amy glanced up from the paper crown she was stapling onto a piece of purple cloth. Headgear for the three wise men was easy to make. She didn't have to bother Bethany or the other artsy women for these.

"What?" She'd been miffed at Reed's bossy manner earlier when the tree fell, but she was too tired now to fuss at him. She was staying later than usual tonight because she wanted to finish as much as she could. Time was racing past and there were so many details to take care of. She wanted this pageant to be the best one ever, and if that meant longer evenings for her, she was okay with that. Sammy and Dexter were coloring Christmas pictures at the next table, but any minute now she expected one of them to fall asleep.

She paused long enough to look up at Reed. He'd shed his jacket somewhere and a dab of brown paint smudged one cheek. Humor lurked in his walnut-colored eyes.

"I've been watching you for a whole minute and a half and not one person has come in to ask you to solve a problem. You must have put out all their fires."

A half grin tugged at her lips. "Oh. Well, that's my job as director."

"Big job."

"I like doing it. This year is especially important."

"Yeah." He scraped out a chair and straddled it.

Amy went back to her staple job. Weird how the room simmered with fresh energy when Reed entered.

"For Ben," he said.

The energy buzz lessened.

"I didn't mean Ben, although he's a part of it, I guess."

Reed crossed his arms over the top of the chair and leaned his chin on them. Something about the action reminded her of Dexter and Sammy. Had Reed Truscott ever been a little boy? He always seemed so…so manly.

"What *did* you mean?" he asked. His lips barely moved, but enough so that her gaze was drawn to them. They were straight and well formed, with natural brackets around each end. He'd shaved recently, but the dark smudge of whiskers was visible this close.

Amy averted her gaze, returning to her handiwork. Headpieces wouldn't make themselves.

"The treasure has everyone thinking about money instead of the real meaning of Christmas. I want us to bring faith and love and community back to Treasure Creek."

"Did it ever leave?"

She lifted an eyebrow. "Sometimes I wonder."

He must have heard the sigh and the fatigue in her voice, because he said, "You look beat."

She pushed at a strand of hair brushing her cheek. As soon as she released it, the lock tumbled down again. She probably looked more than tired. She looked haggard and old and unattractive. "Flattery."

"Get someone else to do this little stuff." Reed tucked the stray lock of hair behind her ear.

The whisper touch tingled against her skin. "Like who?"

His answer surprised her more than his touch. "Me."

She held up a staple gun and a strip of purple cloth. "You want to staple the wise men's crowns?"

"Think I can't?" He took the materials from her. Their fingers brushed. Another tingle, warm and pleasant, danced on her fingertips. All this tingling...what did it mean?

Fatigue, she figured. "Well...thanks. If you staple these, I can write up the program."

She started to push back from the table, but Reed caught her hand. The tingle, more like electricity now, moved up her arm.

"Sit."

Amy thought about protesting. She thought about telling him she could take care of herself. But she was tired, and in his take-charge way, Reed was trying to be kind.

"Things won't get done if I don't do them."

"How about you let me get you a cup of apple cider and you rest a minute."

"I can sip cider while I write."

But her protest came too late. Reed was up and over to the counter and back again in an efficiency of movement. For a big guy, he moved with the grace and speed of a shark.

He set the cup in front of her and pushed back his sleeve to reveal his watch. "Two minutes."

Amy tilted her head, puzzled. "What are you talking about?"

"You are going to sit still for two minutes, relax and drink that cider."

"Or what? You gonna arrest me?" Before Ben's death, she and Reed had been good friends. The ill-begotten proposal had raised a hedge between them and she missed the silly give-and-take they'd once shared.

At her cheekiness, Reed grinned. Breath clogged in Amy's chest. He scowled and grumbled at her so much, she'd forgotten about his killer grin.

"Could."

"What's the charge?" she asked, sipping at the hot, spicy drink.

"Resisting an officer. Disturbing the peace."

"Hey, I'm not bothering a soul. Whose peace am I disturbing?"

His eyes narrowed into slits, but the dark brown irises twinkled. "Mine."

A light, airy, completely bewildering feeling ballooned inside Amy as she contemplated the remark. She fought down the response, deciding she was more tired than she had thought. She reached for the staple gun. A big hand beat her to it.

"Uh-uh." Reed tapped his watch, the corner of his mouth lifting just a little. "One more minute."

He took over the staple job, working without a word. That was Reed's way. Quiet. Steady. Capable. She remembered when he and Ben were working on the house, Ben would be talking about hunting or God or the next extreme tour. Reed would occasionally add a word or a grunt and go right on hammering and sawing. He wasn't big on conversation.

The stapler *click-clacked.* Reed held up a headpiece. "How's this?"

"Perfect. Is my time up?"

Reed's grin widened. "Fidgety, aren't you?"

"I like to keep busy."

"So I noticed."

He had? Well, of course he had. Reed considered her his duty, a thought that chaffed more each time they met. They were friends. He shouldn't feel as if she were a responsibility. He should feel—well, she wasn't sure what he should feel, but definitely not duty.

"Time's up." He pushed the pad and pen toward her and reached for the final crown and strip of cloth. The small garment looked fragile in his large, capable hands. Hands that could take care of a whole town.

"So, what did you think?" she asked.

"About?"

She shrugged. "The pageant. Church."

"Noisy." When she glared at him in mock anger, he grinned that grin again. "Not bad. I kind of liked it."

"Will you come back? Maybe on Sunday?"

One strip of eyebrow arched. "Got to."

"Oh." She understood. "You don't have to guard me day and night."

"I know." *Click-clack.* The final staples went in. If he said Ben would expect it, she would be tempted to staple his lips together. Instead, he asked, "How are the boys doing? Sammy seems nervous."

The fact that he brought up her boys took the arch out of her spine. "He is. I don't know what to do about it, either. The break-in scared him so badly. Maybe if you reassured him, he'd feel better."

"Me?" Reed looked as if she'd asked him to eat whale blubber.

"You're the police chief. Big and brave. I just thought..." She shrugged.

Reed carefully folded the headpiece and laid it aside. "If you think it would help."

Amy brightened. "I do."

"Well, okay." He looked none too confident, a fact that amazed her. Reed always seemed sure of everything.

"Will you watch the boys for one minute while I go get something? I left the song list in the sanctuary."

"Sure." He reached for his own cup of cider and sipped, watching her over the rim.

After a quick word to the boys, who seemed fine with Reed as their momentary babysitter, Amy exited the fellowship hall and nearly collided with Ethan Eckles. The pianist caught her by the arms. Like most of the men in Treasure Creek, Ethan was young, single and not bad-looking. Any number of the new women in town had tried to cozy up to the elementary school teacher, but so far he'd remained aloof.

"I thought you might need the song list," Ethan said, indicating the paper in his left hand.

Amy laughed. "Great minds run together. I was just heading your way."

"Yeah?" He looked especially pleased. Amy's attention went to the inch-long keloid scar along Ethan's left cheekbone and wondered where the quiet, peaceable man had gotten it. Not on one of her tours, she was certain.

"I thought you'd be gone by now," she said. "Practice went better than usual tonight."

The scar puckered as he smiled. "I was putting the finishing touches on 'Mary, Did You Know?'"

"I love that piece. Karenna's soprano is perfect for it."

"I think so, too."

"Well, thanks," she said, expecting him to turn and leave. He didn't. Instead, Ethan shifted on one booted foot and then the other. Then he cleared his throat.

"Look, Amy, I was thinking."

About to turn, she paused, head tilted. "About the pageant?"

"About supper." He patted his flat belly. "I thought you might want to go down to Lizbet's when we finish up here. I want to talk to you about something."

"About the pageant?" Okay, so she was repeating herself. Ethan worked for her, for goodness' sake. And she felt ages older. But okay, he was great-looking. And nice. And smart. And as tough as any of her guides.

"We could talk about the pageant if you wanted. And other things."

She was not going to ask what other things he had on his mind. She liked Ethan. He was a great guy. And he was the first man who'd approached her that she'd actually considered going out with. But was she ready for this?

"It's getting late, Ethan."

"Have you eaten?"

"Well, no, but my boys have, and they need to be in bed soon. Maybe another time?" Had she really said that?

"You need to eat, Amy. Come on. What do you say? Let a friend buy you a burger. We won't stay long."

While she was contemplating the very pleasant idea of letting a nice man buy her dinner, she felt movement behind her. A grouchy voice interrupted.

"Is there a problem out here?"

Chapter Five

Reed's neck muscles were as tight as fishing line. Ethan Eckles was looking at Amy as if she were a delectable bite of T-bone steak. Any minute now, he'd probably ask her to marry him or something.

"Reed!" Amy's eyes widened and their expression went from interested to annoyed.

"I thought you were going after a song list," he said, feeling like a grumpy father spying on his daughter. Check that. Not like a father. What he felt was dark and inappropriate and a lot like jealousy.

"Ethan was kind enough to bring it to me."

Reed's boots squeaked as he shifted. He did not want her going out with Ethan Eckles. Ben wouldn't like it.

Face it, Truscott. You're not thinking of Ben.

"Well, now you have it," he said, fighting down the inner voice. "Let's go."

Eckles had the gall to speak up. His quiet voice was calmer than Reed felt. "I'll see her safely home, Chief. Don't worry."

Don't worry? He did nothing but worry when it came to Amy and the boys.

"Keeping an eye on the town is *my* job. The boys need to

be in bed." The two comments had little to do with each other, but he was sinking fast and didn't know how to stop.

Stubborn sparks glittered in Amy's blue eyes. "If you're so concerned, why aren't you watching them like I asked?"

Reed looked over one shoulder. The two boys were headed his way. "I am."

Dexter and Sammy arrived and stopped directly in front of Reed, not Eckles, who they knew from school as well as church. Reed experienced a certain sense of satisfaction in their choice.

"Do you like my picture?" Sammy asked, shoving the page toward Reed.

Reed went down on one knee to examine the artwork. The Wise Men were decorated with a scribble of red and blue. The camels were purple. "Looks great." Awful. "You ready to go home?"

Amy cut him off. Her tone was colder than a Nome January. "Boys, get your coats. Ethan is taking us to Lizbet's for a late supper. Isn't that nice?"

Reed ground his teeth together and rose to his full height. He was a good three inches taller than the piano-playing schoolteacher. Amy didn't seem to notice.

Before Reed could think of a way to keep her from leaving, Amy had gathered her boys and, with a smile at Ethan Eckles that soured Reed's stomach, left the church.

The Alaska's Treasures office sang with activity. The phone rang, a fax machine burred, and the smell of coffee and fresh cinnamon rolls filled the air. Amy peeled a still-warm bun from the aluminum pan and carried it with her to the table in the back where her staff was gathering for the monthly meeting. All the regulars were there, although some of the part-timers, like Alex Havens, the local pediatrician, and Ethan were not present.

The thought of Ethan Eckles brought back the recent night of play practice. She felt a little guilty going out with him when she'd been ready to refuse. It was Reed Truscott's fault. If he hadn't interfered she'd never have gone. But he had, and to tell the truth, she'd had a good time. Ethan was kind to the boys and easy to talk to. Several times at Lizbet's, she'd held her breath, afraid he was going to do something stupid like too many other men in Treasure Creek and insist she marry him for her own good. But he hadn't. Maybe that's why she'd enjoyed herself. He hadn't insulted her with an awkward, condescending proposal.

Unlike Reed Truscott.

"Amy?"

Aware she'd been woolgathering, Amy brought her attention back to the staff gathered around the long conference table. Casey was gazing at her with an odd expression.

"What? Did I miss something?"

"Nate asked if you had a confirmation on the dogsledding tour."

"Oh." Amy quickly shuffled through the file lying on the table in front of her. "Yes. The deposit arrived yesterday. A party of six."

Nate scribbled something on a yellow tablet. "Mind if I take Bethany along on this one?"

Smiles and sideways glances passed around the table. Since falling hard for the town's wedding planner, Nate kept his tours short to spend more time with Bethany. The dogsledding tour lasted a week—too long for the love-smitten rancher to be away from his fiancée.

"It's your tour, Nate, and Bethany is an able guide, as well. As long as there are other women along—"

Nate's head snapped up. He frowned. "Wouldn't take her if there weren't."

Amy bit into the cinnamon bun with a smile. Yes, indeed, her guide had it bad for Bethany.

As she looked around the table, she realized that several of her guides had fallen in love during the last few months. As happy as she was for them, Amy suffered an unwelcome twinge of envy. Even with her sons for company, her little old house grew lonelier by the day.

Maybe she'd accept Ethan's offer of another dinner. *Maybe.* He didn't set off sparks behind her eyeballs the way Ben had, but he was companionable. Good-looking too, in a blond, Norwegian way. Then again, maybe she shouldn't. She wasn't husband hunting, regardless of Ben's request, and leading Ethan on wasn't fair.

She sighed and gnawed at the end of a pen.

Perhaps she was being oversensitive. After all, Ethan had asked her to dinner, not to marry him. Thank goodness. He was no more ready to wed than she was.

At the same time, she was lonely, and the loving looks and obvious joy floating around the office had her wishing for someone of her own again.

Not that anyone could replace Ben. But widows did love again. They *did* remarry happily. Not for protection or because they couldn't live without a man, but for love. Reed should have thought about that before he'd made his ill-advised proposal. What was wrong with him, anyway? He was a friend. He should have known better than to ask her to marry him for Ben's sake. If she ever married again, it would be for love, not because Ben wanted her to.

"Amy. Amy, are you all right?" This time the receptionist, Rachel, had placed a hand on Amy's. "You seem really distracted this morning."

Embarrassed to be caught woolgathering again, especially about Reed Truscott, Amy reached for her coffee and took a big swallow. The hot liquid seared her tongue. "Sorry. Tired, I guess."

"Well, you do too much." Rachel patted her. "And eat too little."

"You sound like Reed." The moment his name slipped between her lips, Amy wished it back. A hush fell over the table. She glanced around at faces alive with curiosity. "I mean, he's always nagging me to take better care of myself."

"Hmm," Rachel said, lips pursed.

"Interesting," Casey said, head tilted and brown eyes dancing.

"He has an overactive sense of duty."

"Is that what it is?" Casey asked.

Amy gripped the pen so hard she thought it might snap. "What else could it be?"

"He sure is hanging around here a lot lately." This from Andy Carlson, the "old man" in the group. With his experience traipsing the hills and trails as a former postal worker, Andy led many of the backcountry hunting and fishing tours.

"All of you know the reason Reed hangs around all the time. The treasure. And Ben."

At the mention of Ben, the speculation ceased. A dozen pairs of eyes slid away. Feeling a little guilty about injecting Ben as means to stop the silly undercurrent about Reed and her, Amy shuffled through her file again. She liked Reed. They were friends. *Friends.* But the heat in her cheeks didn't go away.

"Now let's discuss finances. Gage's winter adventure tour not only brought in enough to make payroll, it brought us two more bookings. With the other tours set up for the holiday, we're slowly getting our legs under us again."

"We had an inquiry yesterday about one of Casey's 'rugged woman' treks. A women's club out of Minneapolis." The phone in the front office began to ring. Rachel jumped up. "Sounds like more business."

As the receptionist bustled from the room, Amy turned her focus to Casey. "Have you had a chance to talk to the women's group yourself?"

"I'll call the contact number when we finish here."

"Good. Now, let's see…" She flipped a page just as Rachel rushed back into the conference room, eyes wide.

"Amy, it's for you." She held out the cordless phone. "The preschool."

Rachel's tone was tense. So was her expression. A skitter of concern ran through Amy. "My boys?"

Wide-eyed, Rachel nodded. Every single guide at the table stood up. Fighting panic, Amy grabbed for the telephone. Had something happened to Dexter or Sammy?

When Amy arrived at the preschool a record four minutes later, Reed and his amiable dog waited in the pastor's office along with the pastor's wife, Jenny Michaels, and the boys. Even though Pastor Ed had assured Amy the boys were fine, other than being a little upset, the fact that Reed was here indicated there was more to the story than she'd been told.

Dexter was sitting beside the police chief, with his short little legs sticking straight out from a vinyl chair and one hand resting on Cy's noble head. His snow boots gleamed with moisture, indicative of his time outside at recess. His eyes were red as if he'd been crying. Most telling of all was the fact that he was attached to Reed's side like a barnacle. Sammy sat on Jenny's lap, but leaped down the moment he spotted his mother. He ran to her, thumb in his mouth. She caught him up in her arms.

"What's going on, Pastor? Reed? On the phone you said someone was talking to them through the playground fence and scared them."

"That's right, Amy." The pastor rose from behind his desk. "Have a seat."

Fidgety to know what the big deal was, Amy perched on the edge of a hard chair, still holding baby Sammy. He leaned his warm, rosy-cheeked face against her neck and sighed.

"Who scared my boys? And why?"

"Well, that's the problem. We're not sure who the men were."

"Men?" The hair on the back of her neck tingled. "How many?"

"Two. Jenny had playground duty, and spotted two men at the fence talking to Dexter." Pastor Ed looked toward his wife, who nodded in confirmation.

"I started toward them immediately," Jenny said, "but by the time I arrived, they had hurried away."

"Did you know them?"

"No, but I got a fairly good look at one."

Amy turned her focus to her son. "Who was it, Dex? Did you know them?"

Her son hiked both shoulders. "Bad guys."

Amy's gaze jerked toward Reed. His scowl was fierce... and worried.

"Did you know their names?"

"Nuh-uh."

"Then how do you know they were bad? Maybe they were just lost and needed directions. Or maybe one of them was someone's daddy, looking for one of the other children."

Dexter's cleft chin jutted with determination. "Nuh-uh. They were bad."

Reed's long legs rotated until his knees bumped Dexter's boots. His voice was gentle. "What did they say? What scared you?"

Her son's lips begin to quiver. Sympathetic Cy moved

closer to nuzzle Dexter's side and stare up at him with a worried gaze.

"They asked about Mama's treasure chest. The smelly man said he knew I could tell him. If I did he'd give me candy."

Amy's heart fell. The treasure again. *Lord, if I didn't truly believe You wanted me to wait until Christmas, I would open it now. Or maybe throw that box in the river and forget about it.*

Reed leaned forward. "What did you tell the smelly man?"

"I told him I don't know. I don't know where it is." Dexter's voice rose to a frightened wail and fat tears trickled down his face.

Amy could stand it no more. With a son on one hip, she knelt in front of the other. Sammy wiggled loose to embrace his crying brother and the furry, fretting malamute.

"You're okay, baby. You did the right thing."

"He's still upset about something, Amy. Let the boy talk."

Amy wanted to tell Reed to take a dip in the Arctic Ocean, but she refrained. He was right. Something else was bothering her son. "Tell us, Dex. What did the bad man say?"

Dexter's face crumpled. "He said he was gonna get me and Sammy. He'd get you, too. And you would be sorry."

Then her oldest baby fell against Reed and began to sob. Amy wanted to sob, too. At the same time, she wanted to hunt the man down and wring his horrid neck. Her insides shook with the thought that someone had threatened her children.

Over the top of Dexter's head, Reed's gaze met hers. Fury burned in his walnut-colored eyes. Quietly, he said to Amy, "Mrs. Michaels gave me a pretty good description of one of them. I'll ask around town. Maybe someone has seen him. Could be someone even knows him."

It was creepy to think Dexter's tormentor might be someone she knew. "Okay."

But in the meantime, how did she ensure her sons' safety? If anything happened to Dexter or Sammy, she couldn't go on breathing.

"This is a terrible situation, Amy," Pastor Ed said. "I can promise you we will do everything possible here at the church and the preschool to make certain no one enters the playground or school without a visitor's pass and careful scrutiny."

They'd never before had to do such a thing in safe little Treasure Creek. "Thank you, Pastor. I'm really concerned about this."

"Rightly so. Let's pray a prayer of protection over you and the children right now."

"Yes. Please." She took her son's hands and bowed her head while Pastor Ed prayed a simple, heartfelt prayer. Reed's knee brushed her arm as he squirmed. Did prayer make him nervous?

"Amen."

"Amen," she murmured and opened her eyes to find Reed staring at her. Warmth spread up her back, and though she willed it away, her peach complexion heated, too. Why was he looking at her with such intensity?

"I'll see you and the boys safely out," he said.

"Don't you have more investigation to do?"

"Finished." He rose, easily lifting Dexter into his arms.

By now Dexter's tears had stopped, but he sniffed and shuddered into a tissue Jenny had given him.

After a few more comments to the others present, Amy followed Reed and his dog out into the cold, gray day.

She turned toward the parking lot and her SUV, reluctant to be alone. "I'm parked near the front."

"I'm in back." Yet he didn't relinquish Dexter.

"Reed," she started.

"Amy." He faced her, stance spread in the crusty snow like a gunfighter of old. A bill cap bearing the police emblem shaded his eyes. "You can't go home."

She said nothing, simply remained there in the crisp December air, holding Sammy close. She'd never been afraid of anything, but now, with her babies threatened, she tasted a fear so profound it nearly took her to her knees.

"You understand that, don't you?" Reed insisted. "You have to pack up and move to my place until this is over."

"I can stay with Casey."

"She can't protect you the way I can."

He was right. Casey would try, but Reed was the police chief. He was trained to protect people. He was trained to know the good guys from the bad guys.

Sammy's baby breath puffed against her neck, warm and moist. He was asleep on her shoulder, depending on her to take care of him.

Lord, what should I do?

"Will you get them, Chief Reed?" her other son asked, arms wrapped around Reed's neck as though he'd never let go. "Will you?"

Most men would have quibbled. Reed simply clenched his jaw and said, "Yes."

Amy knew he meant that single word with everything in him. She also knew she had her answer. Regardless of how uncomfortable she might feel about moving into his house as a guest, Reed would protect her sons.

And that was all that mattered at the moment.

With Reed rambling around down below like a suspicious cop, Amy was upstairs in her blue house, packing for the temporary move to the police chief's ranch. She knew the decision would cause speculation, but that was the least of her concerns today. Although she planned to be in town on a regular basis and could come by anytime for other items, she wanted to take the things that mattered most to her and the boys. Right now, they all needed the comfort of familiar, well-loved belongings.

Opening the top drawer of her dresser, she withdrew a packet of letters. She'd found them after Ben's death, both ouched and crushed to know he'd written a secret love letter o her before every wilderness excursion. "Just in case," each etter said. She knew what he meant. Just in case he didn't eturn.

She smoothed open the last letter, taking comfort in the amiliar scribble of Ben's handwriting. Before that particular excursion, he'd been increasingly worried about the struggling economy and the subsequent decline in their tour business. The wild river tours had been his way of generating extra funds, though he was acutely aware of the danger. But Ben was safety-conscious and an excellent guide. Concern for his customers had caused his death, not recklessness.

Her gaze roamed over the familiar words. She'd read and reread the letter until the paper had become limp. His previous letters were filled with love and bubbling with the joy of the Lord and their lives together. This last one was different, as though his spirit was heavy with the secret knowledge that he would not return.

"It's still Christmastime. The Lord has given me everything I could ever want—my beloved family. If I don't come home to you, my sweet Amy, your gift to me is that you and the boys won't spend the next Christmas alone. Christmas is for families and little boys need a father."

Tears welled in Amy's eyes as they always did. Was Ben looking down from Heaven this very moment, speaking to her through his letter, urging her to remarry?

She'd pondered the words many times. In the past, she'd been repulsed by the idea. Today she felt nothing but sadness at the loss of a good husband and a fine man. Maybe someday she would find love again. She wanted to. She was still young and her heart ached with such loneliness at times that she cried out to God for comfort.

Her thoughts went to Reed Truscott.

Childish giggles rose up the staircase and filtered in through her open bedroom door. A low rumble of Reed's voice followed.

Amy listened for a moment, feeling safe and protected.

Reed Truscott would marry her tomorrow if she asked, but she wouldn't. If she ever remarried, it would not be for protection, nor for a father for her boys, nor for her business or for any other reason except the God kind of love she'd shared with Ben.

Reed's voice intruded again. She listened, heart lifting oddly at the strong, warm sound.

She shut the door and kept on packing.

His proposals had been clear. They should marry because Ben expected him to take care of her.

But Amy James wouldn't settle for less than love.

Chapter Six

His house felt different.

Reed paused in the doorway between the living room and kitchen to watch his houseguests. He'd just arrived home from a late shift, but wasn't nearly as tired as he'd been of late. Probably because he didn't need to worry so much about Amy. She was here in his house, safe and protected the way Ben would want.

At the moment, she and her sons were ensconced on his navy-plaid couch, one boy on each side of the mother, staring at an enormous picture book. A fire snapped in the fireplace and added an amber glow to the cozy scene. A puzzling mix of tension and contentment swirled around inside him like scented candle smoke.

From the time two days ago when Granny had opened the rarely used dormer floor for the use of his guests, Amy, Dexter and Sammy had taken over his home in the most interesting way. He was accustomed to very quiet evenings and a spotless house. Though the boys were ordinary little boys, they were noisy and active. Reed had stepped on more than one tiny metal car in his sock feet and had gone around hopping with his teeth gritted. Granny Crisp had laughed at him.

The truth was, he liked having them here, no matter what.

He must have made a noise, because all three of the little family looked up from the book and caught him watching them.

Amy's bow mouth curled in a smile. "Hi."

"Hi." Stupid thing to say. But he'd never been glib of tongue with women. Not that he considered Amy a woman. Well, she was, but not in that way. Whatever way he meant. She was Ben's widow.

The constant reminder poked like a sticker in his sock.

He crossed to the fireplace and spread his hands over the heat. "Cold outside."

Another stupid comment. This was Alaska. In December. Of course it was cold outside.

"Not as bad as it could be."

His shoulders relaxed. She wasn't making fun of him. He turned around. "True."

December had been kind so far.

"You want to read with us, Chief?" Dexter's gray eyes searched him.

"Yeah, come read with us." Sammy was snuggled under his mother's right arm.

"What are you reading?" he started toward the trio, unsure of the protocol. Had anyone ever read to him when he was small? He barely remembered his mother. His father certainly hadn't, and he hadn't come to live with Granny until he was too old for story time.

"*Rudolph.*" Dexter patted the couch cushion next to him. Reed sat.

Before he was well settled, Dexter was on his lap. Warmth crept into Reed. He didn't much know what to do with kids, but these little boys belonged to Ben, and he didn't want to let them down. He snaked his left arm around Dexter's middle and was pleased when the child leaned back against him, snuggling in for the read.

Cy, who'd trailed in with his master, circled three times before coming to rest on the rug in front of the fireplace. He sighed softly as he rested his snout on his feet. His eyebrows twitched as his one-eyed, golden gaze volleyed between his master and the two little boys.

Dexter strained toward the open pages of *Rudolph,* pulling against Reed's hold. "I can't see the book, Chief."

"Oh, sorry." Reed started to withdraw his arm and move away, but Dexter clamped on like a vise.

"No, Chief. Scoot."

Scoot? As in closer to Amy? His pulse jumped. He cleared his throat.

No use making a big deal of it. Reed scooted until Dexter could see the pictures of reindeer frolicking in the snow. The action trapped Reed's right arm, smashing his shoulder against Amy. She didn't appear to notice, but he certainly did. After a few seconds of painful indecision, while his loyalty to Ben warred with having Amy this close, he slid his arm over the back of the couch. Her long hair tickled the back of his hand. He could smell her Christmas-cookie scent, mixed with the warm body heat of little boys and the rich fragrance of food coming from Granny's kitchen.

"Can you see all right?" Amy asked, tilting her head toward him.

"Fine." He cleared another unexpected frog from his throat. "Can you see, Dexter?"

"Yep. Read, Mama. I like this part."

Amy began to read about the reindeer refusing to let Rudolph play with them. Sammy's thumb popped out of his mouth. "I feel sorry for Wudolph."

"Me, too," Dexter said. "Why won't they let him play? He's nice."

"Because he's different," Amy said. "See, boys, this is why you should always treat people nicely, no matter how they look. We're all different on the outside. It's the inside that matters. God looks at your heart, not at your nose."

She tapped Dexter's nose and rubbed her face against Sammy's. Both boys giggled.

Leave it to Amy to weave a Bible lesson into the story of a flying reindeer. She went back to reading. Reed listened to the gentle rhythm of her sweet voice, thinking how lucky Sammy and Dexter were to have Amy James for a mother. When she closed the book, he was surprised to find the story over, and even more surprised at his reluctance to move away from the cozy little family.

Family.

Granny Crisp sashayed in through the front door, letting in a waft of cold air. He had no idea where she'd been.

"You two." She pointed at Dexter and Sammy. "Come with me."

"Is it a surprise, Granny?" Dexter had already figured out that she was a cupcake who usually had something entertaining up her sleeve. It might be a cookie—a surefire favorite—or a new game or even a cocoon she'd found stuck to the inside of the garage. The latest of these was in a jar on the mantel, awaiting spring.

"You never know until you come." Granny whipped off a pair of "bunny boots"—big, fat, white rubber boots that kept her feet warm up to temperatures of sixty below—and in brown thermal socks, traipsed off toward the back of the house. Dexter and Sammy hopped down and followed. Cy tailed them, fluffy tail wagging.

"The Pied Piper," Amy said, smiling at the back of her boys.

"In thermal socks." Which put him in mind of Amy's socks. She seemed to have a hundred pair of crazy things to wear on her feet. Tonight, the socks were glittery silver, with red bells and green pom-pom balls. He knew, because her feet were propped on the ottoman right in front of him.

At that moment, he realized he was still sitting close to her on the couch. Real close. And the boys and the book were gone. He should move away. He didn't.

He cleared his throat again. Must be coming down with something. "I wanted to talk to you without the boys anyway."

Amy shifted, pivoting her body so that her back was against the couch arm and she was facing him. With firelight flickering in her hair and against her skin, she was golden and beautiful. Too beautiful for a guy like him.

"Is it about the men at the school? Did you find out who they were?"

"No, but Casey recognized the description."

"Casey? How?"

"One of the descriptions matched the man she saw on the trail."

"The one who tried to take the map?" She pushed at a lock of hair.

Reed resisted the urge to help. "One and the same."

"At least we have a description now. We can spread the word, and everyone in town can stay alert in case the man comes lurking again."

"I'm way ahead of you. Casey did a sketch. It's rough, but good enough, I think."

"Good." She turned her head to stare into the fire. The light caught in her red hair and danced in rhythm with the flickering flames. She had such pretty hair. He thought again about touching it to see if it was as soft as it looked, but resisted. She was his guest, not his girl.

The thought caught in his brain and repeated like a CD on continuous play. She wasn't his girl. But he'd asked her to be his wife.

Oh, Ben, what did you do to me?

He started to get up, but Amy said, "How was your day?" and he resettled.

"Mostly uneventful. Boring."

She laughed. "It's been a while since you could say that."

His mouth twitched and he relaxed more. He and Amy had been friends for years. *Friends.* He needed to remember that. "Calm before the storm."

"Pessimist." She wrinkled her nose at him. She was so cute when she did that. "Maybe the storm is over."

She was teasing, and he liked it. Trouble was, he had no snappy comeback. "I hope you're right."

A log fell in the fireplace, shooting sparks and drawing their attention. They watched the glow for several seconds of comfortable silence.

"Great socks."

"Yeah?" She wiggled her toes. "Want me to buy you a pair for Christmas?"

"If word got out that the police chief wore jingle bells on his socks, no one would take him serious."

"It could be our little secret."

Her blue eyes sparkled up at him and pleasant warmth ballooned in his chest. Again, he fought the urge to touch her. A touch might do him in. "We already have one, remember?"

"How could I forget? Hopefully, no one else finds out you keep the treasure chest hidden at the police station."

"It's safe there. Don't worry." He might tell her not to worry, but he worried every second. If anything happened to Amy's treasure, she and the town would be crushed. They'd pinned so many hopes and dreams on the mysterious contents of one small box. "Only a couple of weeks left until we can finally see what's inside that chest and put this whole thing behind us."

"Or in front of us," Amy said with her insistent optimism.

"Haven't you noticed how the townspeople have become energized with the excitement? For a while there, they'd been too glum to decorate for the holidays, and now we're having a big decorating bash the week before Christmas. For all the problems it's caused, the treasure is a good thing."

Amy was certain God wanted to bless the town through whatever was inside that treasure chest. Reed sure hoped God didn't let them down.

"I guess you'll be right in the middle of the town decorations."

"Won't you?"

"Wouldn't miss it." As the town's peace officer, he couldn't. Plus, he'd have to keep an eye on Amy and the boys. "You want to watch some TV?"

"No. I like sitting here looking at your fire, thinking." She rubbed her upper arms.

"I'll put more wood on."

He started to rise, but Amy caught his elbow. "The fire is fine, Reed. Sit and relax. You work hard."

That simple little comment had a strange effect on Reed Truscott. He sat down again, this time putting more space between him and Amy so that he could look at her while they talked. Self-torture, but worth the pain. "So do you. I'm surprised you aren't working on a costume or something."

"As a matter of fact..." She reached down beside the end of the couch and pulled up a basket of Christmas balls. "Do you like them?"

"Sure." He frowned at a bright, shiny red ball decorated with lace and glitter. "What are they?"

Amy giggled. "I'm personalizing the decorations for your Christmas tree."

"What?"

"The boys and I want a Christmas tree." She pointed at an empty corner of the room. "Right over there."

"I never put up a tree."

"You've never had two little boys underfoot, either. We need a tree, Reed."

Did she say "we"?

"Well, okay," he said uncertainly. Kids expected a tree. Why hadn't he thought of that? Amy and the boys weren't going anywhere until after Christmas, which meant they would have Christmas morning right here in this room. Sweat broke out on his neck. Would he be expected to play Santa? Not that he minded. In fact, he kind of liked the idea, but what exactly did Santa do?

"Let's cut our own." Amy was like a dog with a meaty bone, and her boundless energy had kicked in again. She hopped up from the couch. "What do you say? Are you too tired? We could go now."

Like a family, he thought. He and Amy and Dexter and Sammy traipsing through the woods with a big, green pine, like something from a Norman Rockwell painting.

He gazed down at the bouncy redhead looking up at him with that excited expression and had the strongest urge to pull her into his arms. He might even kiss her, and they'd laugh together in anticipation of the tree they were going to put up. Then they'd bundle the boys and hold hands as they headed into the woods for the perfect Christmas tree. Their first together.

Amy's cell phone rang, a discordant jangle that jarred some sense into him. This was Ben's family, not his.

"No," he said and turned away, but not before he saw the light die on Amy's face.

"Hello." As she spoke into the receiver, Amy kept one eye on Reed, who'd gone from friendly and teasing to stony-eyed and crabby faster than Rudolph's nose could blink.

What was it with this guy? Did he hate Christmas trees?

Well, he might as well get over that, because her children were going to put up a tree. And Mr. Cranky was going to help. He might even like it.

"Amy?"

Amy yanked her focus to the voice coming through the phone. "Yes. This is Amy. Who is this?"

"Ethan."

"Oh, hi, Ethan. How are you?"

Reed, who had started out of the living room, pivoted to glare in her direction. She cocked her head to one side and raised an eyebrow. He narrowed his dark eyes, watching her like a cougar watches a deer. Feeling ornery, Amy made the angled shape of a tree with an index finger and pointed toward the window.

Reed shook his head. "No."

She made a face at him. They were getting a tree.

"Sorry, Ethan," she said, holding Reed's stubborn stare with one of her own. "What were you saying?"

"Heard you moved out to Reed Truscott's ranch." Ethan's tone was casual, but she detected a note of disapproval.

"Until after Christmas."

"Why? Is something wrong?"

She told him about the threat. He hissed through his teeth. "I don't like the sound of that."

"Me, either. That's why I'm here."

"No other reason?"

The question caught Amy off guard. Her gaze faltered, falling away from Reed's ruggedly handsome face. She turned her back, suddenly uncomfortable, though she couldn't pinpoint the reason.

She moved toward the fireplace, its heat rising up like warm fingers to caress her skin. She could feel Reed standing behind her, but he hadn't moved.

This evening they'd read together and his arm had pressed

against hers, his breath warm, his woodsy outdoor scent filling her nostrils. But a Christmas tree had been too much to ask.

"Reed is the police chief. Protecting threatened citizens is his duty."

A truth that chaffed like a week in wet boots. She didn't want him to feel responsible, she wanted… Amy wasn't sure what she wanted, but it certainly wasn't duty.

"Okay." Ethan didn't sound as if he quite believed her.

Was he jealous of Reed? It had been so long since any man had showed her that kind of authentic personal attention, she was flustered.

"The pageant is coming together," she said, more for something to say than anything else.

"You're safe with me, Amy."

"I know that."

"Then let me take you out Saturday."

Amy's pulse jumped. "Take me out? Out where?"

"Wherever you say. We could have dinner at Martelli's or we could take a snowmobile up the mountain."

She hadn't done that in a while. Once, she'd guided tours alongside Ben and the other guides, but since the children had come along, she'd kept to the office to be near them. "I haven't been snowmobiling in a long time."

"Let's go then. Will two o'clock Saturday afternoon be all right?"

Did she really want to do this? With him? "I don't know. Let me check and get back to you, okay?"

"Check? With who? Reed Truscott?"

The question rankled. "My schedule."

By now she was out of the mood to say yes. Besides, Ethan worked for her part-time. Mixing business with pleasure might not be a good idea.

But she and Ben had.

Annoyed with her indecision, she turned to find Reed still

standing in the doorway, staring at her. She waved him away, but he didn't budge.

"Hang up," he mouthed.

Amy glared at him, incredulous, and whispered, "Go away."

Ethan's shocked voice responded, "What?"

"Nothing. Never mind. Ethan, I need to go. I'll talk to you later, okay?"

"Check your schedule then, and we'll talk at practice in a couple of days."

"Right. Sure. See you." With relief, Amy clicked the end button. "What was so important that you had to interrupt a personal call?"

"If you're looking for a husband, I already offered. All you have to do is say the word."

Amy's hackles rose. Through gritted teeth, she said, "I am not looking for a husband."

"You barely know that guy."

"Don't be ridiculous. Ethan works for me." She was so annoyed, she whipped around to leave. Reed's voice stopped her.

"I thought we were going out for a tree."

Amy's mouth gaped. "You said no."

He slapped both hands on his hipbones. "I changed my mind."

"So did I." With that, she flounced up the stairs and left him standing.

Reed was still there, hands on hips, staring dumbfounded at the empty stairs, when Granny sashayed through the hall, Sammy and Dexter trailing happily behind. "What did you do? Make her mad?"

"Something like that. Not sure what I did."

"Doofus," Granny said affectionately. "Well, me and the

boys are going out for pizza. You and Amy fend for yourselves." She patted her purse. "Don't worry. I'm armed and dangerous. Nobody is gonna bother Sammy and Dexter with me around."

He didn't doubt that one bit. Granny had taught him gun safety and shooting. She was better with a firearm than most men, a fact that she proved year after year when she bagged a moose and supplied enough meat for months.

"You're going out? But I thought I smelled something cooking."

"For you and Amy." She slid her skinny arms into a coat and yanked the zipper to her chin. "Me and the fellas want pizza. Right, boys?"

"Yep." Both boys nodded. They were bundled so tightly into parkas, their little faces were the only visible skin. "Mama said okay."

Reed glanced upward. Granny had declared the upper half of the house off-limits "on account of propriety" she claimed. Fine with him.

"Apologize for whatever you did and get it over with." Granny pointed a gloved finger at him. "Don't argue with me, either."

She was half his size, but he never argued with Granny. She had more ways to make him miserable—and happy—than a salmon had eggs. Kind of like Amy. While he was pondering his next move, she and Amy's sons headed for the pizza parlor.

The door had no more than snapped shut behind them when Amy appeared at the top of the stairs, still holding the troublesome cell phone. Was she waiting for Ethan Eckles to call again? Or some other guy? Half the men in town had proposed to her in the last six months. So far, she hadn't taken any of them seriously. But she'd seemed interested in snowmobiling with Eckles.

Amy stared him down, sparks shooting from her blue eyes, shoulders squared. "Granny said dinner was ready, and I'm hungry."

So was he. "I'm free Saturday. We'll get the stupid tree."

The sound of Amy's laughter followed him.

Chapter Seven

"Don't apologize just because Granny told you to."

Amy had started down the stairs, drawn by the delicious smell of a casserole filling the house. Granny Crisp was an amazing cook. She was also up to something. Her sudden hankering for pizza with Sammy and Dexter didn't ring true.

"I'm not."

Holding on to the rail with one hand, Amy paused on the bottom step. "You're not apologizing at all, or you're not apologizing because Granny made you?"

"What did I do, anyway?"

Amy snorted. The man was clueless. "Will you really go with us to get a tree?"

"Said I would."

"Don't sound so thrilled. We'll have fun, I promise."

"We're taking the snowmobiles." His tone was a challenge, as though he expected her to argue. She wouldn't. A Christmas tree with all the trimmings was especially important to her and the boys this year. And she was just beginning to realize that Reed needed an extra dose of Christmas himself.

"Great. I'll fix a thermos of hot cocoa. We'll bundle up, sing carols and make a morning of it. It'll be so much fun."

"Fine. Let's eat." He spun on his sock feet and headed toward the kitchen.

As she followed, Amy observed the tense set of Reed's wide shoulders. They had been friends for a long time, and yet she was only just beginning to understand him. Well, maybe not that much, but a little. A man who never put up a Christmas tree was a lonely man. A little sad even, to her way of thinking.

The truth of that hit her right between the eyes. Lonely? Ultrabusy Police Chief Reed Truscott?

A new determination settled into her bones. She, Sammy and Dexter would make Christmas extra special for Chief Truscott, too. It was the least she could do to repay his hospitality and his loyal, if somewhat overbearing, need to take care of Ben's family.

"I'll set the table," she said. Reed was leaned over the oven with a dish towel in hand. "Better use the oven mitt."

He paid her no mind, extracting an oval dish of chicken and rice with the dish towel and a foil-wrapped pack with his bare hand. He juggled the foil packet a couple of times before tossing it onto the counter.

"Stubborn," Amy said, looking up from setting out two plates.

"Takes one to know one." He thumped the chicken dish down in front of her and grinned.

She grinned back. "At least I admit it."

He grunted. This time Amy laughed out loud.

"Are you going out with Eckles again?"

Ah, so that was a problem. "I don't know. He's a nice guy but…"

"He's not Ben."

"I wasn't going to say that, but there'll never be another Ben."

"No." He took two glasses from the cabinet and filled them with water. "I miss him. Must be a lot worse for you."

His admission touched her. "It's getting easier."

Amy was no longer surprised by that fact. It *was* getting easier.

"Good. I'm glad." He handed her one of the water tumblers. "He wouldn't want you to hurt."

"No, he wouldn't." She thought again of that last letter and his request. Ben not only didn't want her to grieve, he wanted her to move on without him.

"He wouldn't be too happy about the recent turn of events, either," Reed was saying. "Somebody threatening his family would have struck a mighty big nerve. He'd kick my backside if I didn't do my best to take care of you."

"You're doing that, Reed, and I'm grateful." Amy added paper napkins from a drawer, her stomach rumbling with eagerness at the warm, homey scents of the kitchen. "Even if I don't act like it sometimes."

He took salt and pepper shakers from the cabinet and set them, along with his water, on the table. "So you're okay with this living arrangement? Here, with me and Granny? I know it wasn't your favorite idea."

Okay with it? With memories of the letter lingering, Amy held her breath, afraid the conversation might lead to another awkward marriage proposal. She was here to protect her babies, not to find a husband. Wasn't she?

"Not in the beginning, but the boys, especially Sammy, seem more secure since we moved in." She paused, fingertips tracing the soft lace on the white tablecloth. "I wish I was enough for them, but I guess I'm not."

"Hey, don't beat yourself up." Reed gave her a gentle bump with one elbow. "They've been through a lot. You're a great mom."

Reed Truscott was not one to hand out compliments like

Santa handed out candy canes. Amy turned to say thanks, but the words died in her throat as their eyes met. Something weird happened in her chest. An expansion, as if her heart was fuller because of his unexpected praise.

Their gazes locked and held for several long seconds. Inside the gruff exterior of Reed Truscott beat the heart of a good man. She wondered if he knew that. She wondered if anyone, particularly a woman, had ever appreciated the real Reed.

Amy placed a hand on his arm. "That means a lot to me, Reed."

He swallowed and took a step back. Her hand fell away. "Dinner's on. Sit."

Just like that, Amy caught a glimmer inside the chief of police. Tenderness made him uncomfortable. The question was why? And what could she do about it? She'd grown up in a household of huggers and touchers, a family that nurtured and loved, and so she'd become the same kind of openly affectionate person. Now she wondered what Reed's childhood had been like.

Thoughtful, she took the chair he held, and the meal commenced with a clatter of dishes and compliments to the missing chef. Even though Amy helped out around the house, Granny Crisp usually had the cooking underway before Amy got home from work.

She moved the conversation to neutral ground: tours she'd booked; the library council they were both on; the Christmas pageant. She was pleased when he said he'd enjoyed Pastor Ed's sermon on Sunday, but she knew better than to push. She'd keep praying and inviting, and the Spirit would do the rest. Before long, they were both chuckling over Granny's recent tree-climbing incident.

"Age will never hold Granny back," Reed said.

"I hope I'm like her when I'm in my seventies."

"I'm not sure the world can handle two like her." The comment was tempered with a smile.

"Do you think the boys asked for pizza, or is she up to something?"

"Up to something," Reed said around a hearty bite of casserole. "Always is."

He ripped off a chunk of bread and reached for the butter. The police chief could pile butter or gravy on everything and not gain an ounce. "She's crazy about Sam and Dexter."

He was right. Granny adored her sons.

"And beneath that sourdough attitude, Granny is a peacemaker. If we fight, she'll force us to make up."

He made them sound like newlyweds. Amy wondered if he thought Granny was trying to push them together—as a couple. She'd seen other subtle signs of matchmaking, but tonight Granny had been especially obvious. She started to ask, then thought better of it. They were having a pleasant dinner. No use bringing up an uncomfortable subject.

"I never intended to fight with you," she said instead.

He made a snorting noise. "You fight with me all the time. If I say yes, you say no."

"And vice versa."

He tilted his head to one side, lips tilted in amusement. "True. You're fun to spar with."

"I am?" She and Ben had never "sparred." But Reed Truscott could get her blood racing faster than anyone. He made her feel energized. Exhilarated. Alive.

Oh, dear.

Amy took a long drink of water, trying to wash down the irrational thoughts that pinged in her brain like BBs. She and Reed had been having dinner together every evening for nearly a week. Granted, the three pizza eaters were usually present, but there was no reason for her to start thinking of Reed as anything but a friend and the local law enforcement.

Certainly not as a man.

But he *was* a man. A strong man with rugged good looks that had more than one of the newly arrived women stopping by the police station for directions or to express their appreciation for the police force with cookies and cakes and telephone numbers.

A smart woman would appreciate the value of a man like Reed Truscott.

The incessant thoughts kept right on pinging. To shut them up, she said, "Well, I'm not sparring with you tonight. What do you want for Christmas?"

He stopped chewing and laid aside his fork, his head tilted to one side as though he couldn't comprehend her language. "What?"

"Christmas? As in a present? What do you want Santa to put under your tree?"

"Told you, I never put up a tree."

"I know that already, but this year you will." She jabbed a finger at him. "You promised."

His lips quivered. "Guess so."

"Don't try to back out now, buddy boy. There will be big trouble if you do."

"Yeah? More sparring?" The quiver became a full-blown grin. An ornery one.

Feeling silly and light, Amy flipped the ends of her hair. "I happen to know the chief of police."

"Heard he was a tough rascal, but fair-minded." Reed rubbed a thumb and forefinger over his chin in mock seriousness. "Handsome dog, too, from all reports."

Amy said, "Ha!" and tossed a wadded napkin at him. Dark eyes sparkling in fun, he caught it with one hand and tossed it back, smacking her lightly on the shoulder.

"This could be war, you know." She bent to retrieve the fallen napkin. When she raised her head again, Reed had made a pile of at least half a dozen napkins wadded into balls next to his now-empty plate. He was rolling yet another into shape, eyeing her with devious intent.

"Wow, you're fast."

"You declared war. A smart man prepares for battle."

Amy grabbed for the napkins, but before she could shape even one, a wad thunked the top of her head. She dove under the table, clutching a handful of napkins.

Suddenly, Reed was behind her pelting her back and shoulders for all he was worth.

Cy, who'd been lying under the table at first, belly-crawled out. His offended expression was absolutely comical.

"Escape while you can, Cy," Amy said, giggling until her return fire was weak and useless.

By now, Reed had run out of napkins and was scurrying around the kitchen in sock feet to retrieve the paper wads. Amy saw her chance and came out from under the table blasting. Reed spun, trying to dodge the volley. His socks slipped and he tumbled down, all six-foot-something sprawling across Granny's linoleum.

Sputtering with laughter while hoping he wasn't hurt, Amy hurried across the room. "You okay?"

She stood over him, looking down into his face. He was grinning.

"I'll be fine in a minute," he said.

When Amy offered a helping hand, he took it—and yanked. Down she went.

He was wide and long and there was no way she could keep from falling directly against him. She heard an "oof" as she caught herself with both hands against his chest and pushed back.

"Now I'm fine," he said.

"You rat."

Serious Reed Truscott laughed harder than she'd ever seen

him laugh. Amy couldn't resist. She stuck a paper wad in his mouth.

Then she hopped up and ran like a turkey on Thanksgiving.

Cy barked once and followed.

Reed's heavy footsteps thundered after them.

"Be careful," Amy called. "You'll fall down again."

A misguided wad of paper was her answer.

He rounded the corner into the living room where she'd taken refuge behind the couch.

"You can run but you can't hide."

She covered her head with both arms, giggling as he peppered her with all the wadded napkins at once.

"Truce! Truce!" she called. "Can't you see my white flag?" With pitiful effort, she waved a wrinkled, unfolded napkin.

"You surrendering?"

"I have to. I'm out of ammo."

"Say 'Uncle.'"

"You are so mean."

Another wad bounced off her ear. "Say it."

Amy giggled. "Uncle."

Reed collapsed on the couch, huffing and puffing.

Amy plopped down beside him with a loud "Whew!"

They were both grinning like kids. She stuck her tongue out at him. "I had my fingers crossed."

He rolled his head in her direction. "Cheater."

This close, she noticed the brackets accenting his mouth and the tiny crinkles at the corners of his eyes. She noticed the outdoorsy scent of him, too, and most of all, she noticed how good she felt to be having so much fun with a man she admired and respected. Reed could annoy and exasperate her like no one else, but tonight he'd made her feel carefree and happy again. Was that a good thing or a bad thing? Amy wasn't sure, but for now she let the worry slide away. For now, they were two friends enjoying time together.

"Why suddenly so serious?"

She shook her head, not about to tell him what she'd been thinking. "Just wondering."

"What? Where you can get something more powerful than paper napkins to pummel me with?"

"Not at the moment. But be warned, I will." She gave him her meanest look. His nostrils flared in amusement. "Actually, I was thinking about Christmas."

He thumped the back of his head against the couch and groaned. "Figures."

"Seriously. Don't you and Granny exchange Christmas gifts?"

"Back to that, huh?"

"Well, do you or not?"

"Not. If I want something, I buy it. She does the same."

"But that's not the point. It's Christmas!" Amy, a devoted Christmas nut, was astonished and horrified. "It's your sworn duty to want something under the tree."

Reed's lips twitched. "Sworn duty?"

"Well, okay, maybe not sworn." Exasperated, she wobbled her head and rolled her eyes. "But we're having Christmas, and you're getting presents. So deal with it."

He stretched his feet out in front of him and folded his hands on his flat belly. Cy ambled over, sniffed his master's toes and lay down. "Okay."

Just like that? No argument? "Start making a list."

He tilted his head. "Now?"

"No time like the present." And then she laughed. "Bad pun. Sorry."

"I'll have to think about it." He nudged her outstretched foot with his. "What do you want, Ms. Claus?"

"I want. I want—" Amy clasped her hands in front of her

and closed her eyes, almost prayerful "—Mack Tanner's treasure to be the answer to the town's problems. My boys to have a wonderful Christmas and not miss their father too much. My employees to be happy and prosperous and blessed by God."

Suddenly, warm, hard fingers wrapped around her clasped hands. Amy's eyes flew open to find Reed watching her with a strange expression. Gently, quietly, he said, "Ben was a lucky man."

"You want to go with us to find a Christmas tree?" Reed leaned casually on the washing machine next to where Granny was busy folding towels into a basket. The laundry load had tripled with the addition of two active children. Amy did laundry almost as often as Granny, but it was an ongoing process. He'd never considered how active a family would be. Or how the addition of one small woman and two much smaller boys could add so much life to his house.

"A Christmas tree?" Granny rubbed a flat palm over a fluffy towel, smoothing it to perfection. "You're putting up a tree this year?"

"I am. Want to come along?"

"Well, for goodness sake." Granny's expression was overly interested. "Who's going?"

As if she didn't know. "Dexter, Sammy, Amy. Kids need a Christmas tree."

If his tone was gruff, Granny wouldn't notice. He was always gruff. After the dinner with Amy the other night, when he'd blasted off his big mouth and said something incredibly stupid, he was downright cranky. What had come over him?

Ah, what was he thinking? He knew what had brought on the sappy comment about Ben being a lucky man. Amy herself. She'd sat there with her eyes closed like a saint—long golden eyelashes brushing her cheeks, while every wish she made, every prayer she breathed was for someone else. Amy's unselfish desire to give to everyone else had gotten to him big-time.

Ben *had* been a lucky man, but Reed shouldn't have said it. And he shouldn't have touched Amy's hand that way. She was soft and velvety smooth, with just enough chill in her fingers to make him want to warm her up. If they hadn't had that paper wad fight and laughed so much, he wouldn't have let his guard down.

Now that he had, he wasn't sure what to do. He didn't want Amy thinking he was trying to take Ben's place. He wasn't. No one could replace Ben. She'd said so herself.

But he couldn't pretend much longer that he felt nothing but friendship and loyalty for Amy James.

"Are you coming or not?" he groused, irritated he was unable to stop thinking about Amy. Because of his promise to Ben, she'd occupied his thoughts for months. Now that she and those clinging, adorable, messy, funny little boys of hers were underfoot day and night, he was a wreck, thinking thoughts he shouldn't think. Behaving in ways he shouldn't behave.

The more time he spent with Amy the more he wanted—

He clenched his jaw. This wasn't about what he wanted or didn't want. It was about doing what was right, about keeping a promise, about duty and commitment.

Granny Crisp, who'd been eyeing him with a searching look, rubbed her elbow. She grimaced, a fake expression if ever he'd seen one. "You're on your own, boy. It's mighty cold, and these old bones of mine..."

Reed made a rude noise. Those old bones, as she called them, did anything they wanted to outside. She might look as skinny, wrinkled and brown as a piece of moose jerky, but last week she'd cut a pile of firewood and stacked it on the porch—all in one afternoon.

"It won't work, so don't try it," he said.

She reached into the warm dryer for another pile of clothes. "Don't know what you're talking about."

"No need to matchmake. I'm going to ask her to marry me."

Granny paused in midfold. "Well, howdy-do."

"Ben wanted me to."

Granny made a noise that sounded like a mix of chain saw and dog growl. "Don't do it."

Almost grimly, Reed said, "Got to."

"Say a word like that to her, and she'll boot you out."

He already had. To his detriment. "It's my house."

"Don't be an idiot."

"Marrying her is the right thing to do." And if he liked the idea of keeping her here a little too much, he'd deal with the guilt.

"Right thing. Wrong reason." With a huff, she pressed her lips tightly together and slammed a corduroy shirt onto the dryer, dinging the metal top with the buttons.

Flummoxed, with his gut twisting in a dozen directions, Reed spun on his heel and went to find Amy and her boys.

Cy spotted a rare snowshoe hare and gave chase, his tightly muscled body agile in the thick, powdery snow.

Dexter shouted, "Rabbit," and churned after the dog. Sammy followed, but his toddler legs tangled, and he toppled facedown, sinking into the frigid, white fluff.

Amy sucked in a gasp of sharp, lung-burning air. "Sammy!"

She'd been dawdling in the bright white morning, soaking up the startling beauty of the snowy evergreen forests against the backdrop of blue sky and majestic mountains.

Reed ambled along beside her, quieter than usual, as if he had something on his mind. She'd been prodding him, talking a mile a minute about socks and hockey and moose hunting, teasing him about the way he drove a snow machine. He'd come back at her a few times, but mostly he grunted. She wouldn't give up, though. She knew how much fun he could be when he let himself go. And she was determined to see Reed Truscott relaxed and happy and having a great time. Christmas was too important—and so was Reed.

The thought would have stopped her in her tracks if not for Sammy's fall. Now, at her baby's muffled cry, adrenaline kicked into high speed and her legs followed suit.

Dexter, a hundred feet ahead, must have heard the anxiety in her voice, because he spun back toward her, snow flying all around him. Cy returned, flying across the powdery terrain, legs stretched out, tail high and wagging. The dog reached Sammy first and began to nudge and whine. Reed, with his long stride, reached Amy's baby next. He put down the chain saw he'd been carrying and yanked the child up into his arms. Snow drifted off Sammy and coated Reed's jacket. It packed the edges of the little boy's hood and caked around his nose and eyes. His cheeks were bright red and tears glistened in his wide, gray eyes. Looking from Amy to Reed and down at Cy, Sammy started to whimper.

"Are you all right?" Amy asked, breathless when she reached the pair. Her hands flew over her child, wiping away snow, dabbing a runny nose with a tissue.

"He's fine, Amy. Kids fall. They get up." Reed spoke as if he was angry.

Amy observed his expression for a split second before realizing something very important about Reed Truscott. He wasn't angry. He was shaken.

"Well, Chief Tough Cop, if you weren't worried, why did you run?"

Reed sniffed. "Smart aleck."

Amy placed a gloved hand on the thickly quilted arm of his coat. "Caring is a good thing. Thank you, Reed."

She reached for Sammy, but the boy wrapped his arms tightly around Reed's neck and clung like plastic wrap. "Chief Weed cawwy me."

"Chief Weed, huh?" Amy cast an amused glance from her son to Reed. "Chief Weed?"

Chief Weed gave a grunting laugh. "Don't get cute."

Amy wrinkled her nose, grinning. "I am cute, and you know it."

She didn't know why she'd said a flirty thing like that, but when he laughed she suddenly felt light and happy.

Reed mumbled a surprising, "Don't remind me," and traipsed off toward a stand of evergreens.

Amy stood with mouth open, watching the police chief's broad back stalk away from her with Sammy balanced on one hip. Did Reed find her attractive? Was that what he meant?

So what if he did? What then?

Dexter tugged on her hand. "Come on, Mama."

Surely she'd misunderstood. Reed had told her time and again that, as Ben's friend, he was duty-bound to look after her.

Reed stopped and turned, waiting for her to catch up. "I forgot the saw."

"Got it." She reached down, but Dexter was already doing his best to lift the heavy piece of equipment. Amy added a hand but let her son pretend to carry the bulk.

They trudged toward Sammy and Reed, but Amy kept her focus on Dexter and the saw, aware that her feelings for Reed Truscott, Ben's best friend, were becoming increasingly complicated. *Was it possible? No, no. Surely not.*

She glanced at the police chief carrying her son across the pristine snow.

Maybe.

When they reached the pair of young males, Reed had slid Sammy to the ground and they were both walking around a stately young spruce.

"What about this one?"

"Beautiful, but kinda big," she said. "Do we have that much room?"

"Hmm. Maybe." Reed tilted his head back and looked up. Amy went to stand beside him, the heat from his body making a warm circle around her.

"Kinda tall."

He glanced down at her, coffee-colored eyes dancing with merriment. "I could always cut a hole in the ceiling."

"A possibility," she said, holding his gaze, that happy, light feeling coming again. "Wonder what Granny would say to that?"

"She'd skin us both. I'd almost do it just to see her reaction." He grinned down at her.

Energy buzzed between them, along with memories of their paper wad battle.

Amy giggled and bumped the side of her head against Reed's shoulder. "Why, Reed, you bad boy."

His grin widened.

Oh, my, Amy thought. *Oh, my. What is going on here?*

"I want that one." Dexter's small voice interrupted.

Amy turned her attention to her son. "What did you find, baby?"

"I want that one over there. See, Mama, it's perfect."

Both adults followed the direction of Dexter's pointing finger.

"That one?"

"Yep." The child raced toward *the* tree, the one in a thousand that had managed to catch his eye. Sammy and Cy followed, eager to examine Dexter's find.

Amy skidded to a stop, a short distance away from where Dexter and Sammy patted the branches of a spindly Sitka spruce. "Uh-oh."

A Charlie Brown Christmas tree.

She and Reed exchanged looks. "Why this one, Dex?"

Dexter, face hopeful, said, "Look at him, Mama. He's sad. He thinks no one will like him because he's different. Like Rudolph."

Ah. Rudolph.

Reed walked around the scrawny six-foot bundle of scraggly, asymmetrical needles. "He has character. I'll give him that."

Amy's heart bumped. What a sweet thing to say.

"Yeah, Mom, he has character."

Though she loved a beautiful, well-decorated tree, this year Amy didn't care if their Christmas tree was made of tin cans, as long as her boys were happy.

"Character is important."

Dexter threw his arms around the prickly tree. "I love it. Can we take him home?"

Reed ran a gloved hand over the needles. "Well watered. Nice and green. We could do worse."

Under her breath, Amy muttered, "How?"

Reed's eyes twinkled, but he remained serious, taking his cue from the ultraserious child. Amy was thrilled at Reed's reaction. He had to believe, as she did, that this was the ugliest tree in the woods, but his thoughtful response to Dexter's choice touched her to the core.

Sammy walked around the tree, head to one side and a fist to his hip, in imitation of Reed. He nodded sagely. "I want him, too, Chief Weed."

Amy pressed her lips together tightly to keep from laughing. Her boys were all business, choosing this tree as though it were the most important thing in the world. Considering all they had been through this year, maybe for them it was.

"Looks like a 'yes' from our evergreen experts," Reed said. "So what do you say, Mom? Is this a Charlie Brown Christmas?"

To tell the truth, they could all take a lesson from the endearing Peanuts character. Besides, she couldn't turn down Dexter's longing to find value in this one lopsided, gapped spruce.

"Nobody knows Christmas like Charlie. Let's go for it."

A whoop of exuberant joy went up from Dexter, followed by a loud, "Yea!" from Sammy.

"Can I cut him down, Chief?" Dexter asked, reaching for the saw at Reed's side. "I'm a good hand with a saw."

Reed scowled at Amy. "You let him use a chain saw?"

"No, of course not. Dexter, you've never used the saw. Why would you say that?"

"Because I'm big now. And this is my special tree." He spread his blue-mittened hands to each side. "Give a kid a chance."

Reed's response was a no-nonsense bark. "A five-year-old has no business with a saw."

Dexter's animated expression fell, and instantly Reed relented. "Tell you what. You stand over here behind me and I'll show you the tricks of the trade. Next year, we'll use the ax. You can help with the chopping. Deal?"

Amy was sure her son had no idea what tricks of the trade were, and she wouldn't even begin to address the "next year" comment, but Dexter said, "Deal."

He moved to stand behind Reed's right side, gray eyes focused on his latest hero and the power tool. Amy carried Sammy safely out of the way.

The engine revved with one quick yank of the pull cord.

Dexter slapped mittens over both ears and ducked behind the bulky police officer as Reed neatly sliced the tree trunk.

When the scrawny spruce toppled to the snow, more loud whoops went up with the spray of snow. Reed put the saw down, grinning at the exuberant little boy. Amy and Sammy joined them for high fives. Then her sons did a victory dance around the felled evergreen, hopping and clapping and whooping for all they were worth.

When the celebration ended, Amy began to sing "O Christmas Tree."

After a few bars, Reed picked up the tune and added his baritone. A warm feeling flooded Amy's being. Without giving the action any thought, she did what came naturally and slipped one arm around Reed's back and another over Dexter's shoulders. She rocked back and forth, keeping rhythm as they sang.

Sammy, not to be left out, sidled up to Reed, who pulled the child against his leg.

"'O Christmas tree, O Christmas tree....'"

A sweet emotion settled over the odd quartet singing at the top of its lungs to the ugly fallen Sitka spruce.

Chapter Eight

This was what Christmas was supposed to feel like.

Reed held one end of a hundred-bulb strand of multicolored lights while Amy twirled in a circle around the tree, looping and draping and humming along with a CD of Christmas carols.

Dexter and Sammy were piddling around, digging in plastic storage boxes Amy had insisted on bringing from her house.

The local chief of police, renowned for his aplomb in difficult situations, was still feeling a little shell-shocked by the morning's events. Shell-shocked and amazingly peaceful and happy. His tension, always present and pinching at the back of his neck, had dissipated as he'd sung Christmas carols, thrown snow at Amy and behaved like a kid out in the woods.

When had he ever done that? When had he ever felt like a kid? Now twice in the space of a week, Amy had reminded him of how good it felt to let go and enjoy himself.

He looked at Amy's boys, so cute and innocent, they made his heart squeeze. They were depending on him to keep them safe, and with God's help he would not fail.

He'd never considered God much, other than to appreciate

the stunning universe He'd created, but Amy was getting to him on that front, too.

Sammy had stuck a red bow on Cy's head and a blue one on his own. Now the pair lay side by side in front of the fireplace, watching the decorations go onto the tree. Sammy's little arm was looped over Cy's back as they snuggled close together. Both dog and boy looked ridiculously happy.

Amy was a fantastic mother, and her kids deserved an equally fantastic father.

Acid filled his stomach. Even if Amy agreed to marry him, he could never be that kind of father. The only father he'd ever known was harsh and hard, expecting too much. And his mother had been dead too long for him to remember any parenting he may have learned from her. He knew nothing about being a good dad like Ben. What if Amy married him and he was like his father? He'd snapped at Dexter out there in the woods. The reaction had been fear, but still, he'd hurt the boy's feelings. What if he was too hard on Dexter and Sammy? What if they grew up resenting him the way he resented Wes Truscott?

Sweat broke out on the back of his neck. Maybe marrying Amy wasn't for the best.

But he'd promised. He groaned.

"What did you do? Poke yourself?"

Amy's voice came from behind the tree. He could see her through the gaps of evergreen-scented green. He could also see her toe socks, a hilarious pair in bright red, with a silly black yarn face. The fringed eyebrows and googly eyes jiggled whenever she walked. He focused on them. Those were fun. His thoughts were not.

"Not enough branches here to hurt anyone," he muttered, knowing the comment would bring a smile. It did. And he felt better.

"Dexter, are you about ready with those ornaments?"

"In a minute." Sitting cross-legged beneath his chosen tree, Dexter was carefully sorting Christmas balls according to color. "I think Herbie should be all different colors. Okay?"

Amy poked her head from behind the tree. Silver glitter from somewhere sparkled on her red hair and forehead. "Herbie?"

"Yep. His name is Herbie. Herbie Christmas Tree."

Amy's pretty mouth curved up in a peach-colored smile. Nobody smiled with as much real pleasure as Amy James. A man could get lost in a smile like that.

Reed squelched the errant, insistent thought. A man's mind could also drive him off the deep end.

"Herbie he shall be," Amy announced.

"Do you always name your Christmas trees?"

Blue eyes twinkling beneath a Santa hat that quoted, "I believe," Amy looked like a red-haired elf.

"Last year we had Angelina. She was a lovely, delicate girl that we draped with pink angel hair."

Reed shook his head. A strange feeling brewed in his chest. He didn't understand the feeling, but it was like thawing fingers and toes—both hot and cold, comforting and painful. "My family never did anything like this."

"Really? Never? No Christmas memories?" She handed him one of the Christmas balls she'd plastered with lace.

He looked at his distorted reflection in the green ball. "I spent most Christmases on a fishing boat, working with my father."

"Even when you were small?" The way she asked touched him.

"My father said Christmas was just a bunch of people making money off God."

She went up on tiptoes, stretching up to hang a sparkly bell. "Do you believe that way, too?"

He shrugged. "I hadn't given it much thought." But he did today. He stuck the green ball on one of Herbie's limbs.

"That's why we cut our own tree and make a big deal out of decorations and church and singing carols. None of those things costs much, but the memories we make last forever. I want that for my boys. I want the real meaning of Christmas, of family love and giving to others and worshipping Jesus to be the focus. Not stuff. Never stuff."

Well, what had he expected from a woman barely in her thirties who mothered an entire town?

He chewed on her response for a while, mentally agreeing that her way was far better than his. Maybe less comfortable, considering how little emphasis he'd put on God or Christmas or family for that matter. He had Granny and Cy and a great job. When had they stopped being enough?

A half hour later the early Alaskan darkness took over. Reed tossed another log into the fireplace while waiting for Amy and the kids to put the final touches on Herbie. The living room had grown dim, but Amy had refused to turn on the lamp, working by the shadowy light from the dining room instead.

"I'm waiting for the big moment," she said, meaning the lighting of the tree.

"Better than a trip to Rockefeller Center."

"Cheaper, too."

"Smaller crowd."

They both laughed over that one. For an Alaskan, ten people was a crowd.

Granny wandered in with mulled cider and popcorn—an action that stunned Reed and delighted the rest. Once the goodies were passed, she took a seat in her bentwood rocker to observe the festivities.

"Reed, do you mind?" Amy asked.

"Mind what?" He dusted the wood chips from his hands.

"Hold Sammy up so he can put the star on top." She extended a lighted silver star. "I can't reach that high."

"This is my year, Chief Weed. I'm big now." Sammy's tiny teeth gleamed. The little boy was sweet as sugar.

"I'd be honored."

Reed lifted the boy easily, holding him steady while Sammy jammed the star onto one of Herbie's branches.

"You're strong, Chief Weed."

A soft place opened inside Reed's chest.

"Looks like we're ready for the finale," he said, holding Sammy against his shoulder a second longer.

Amy took up the light plug, a jumble of connected strands she promised were not a fire hazard. "Drum roll, please."

Dexter and Sammy pretended to drum. Reed did the countdown. "Three, two, one."

Amy pushed the plug into the wall socket. A multicolored light display illuminated the living room and the spruce.

"Herbie's beautiful," Dexter exclaimed, breathing in four-year-old awe.

Amy clapped her hands once, eyes sparkling. "All he needed was love."

"And lots of tinsel," Reed muttered next to her ear.

She spun toward him, grinning. "The secret of a beautiful tree. Lots of decorations."

He wouldn't exactly call the tree beautiful, but Herbie did look a lot better. Respectable. Almost proud.

Reed gave an internal laugh at his fanciful thoughts. Amy and her little family were affecting him in more ways than he'd ever imagined. Some good. Some downright painful.

He moved to the couch and sat, taking up a handful of popcorn and a warm cup of cider.

"We're not finished yet, Chief," Sammy said. "We gots to

hang the weaths and the misting toe and the stockings. Santa puts stuff in our stockings."

While the adults grinned at Sammy's cute butchering of the word *mistletoe,* a solemn Dexter carefully smoothed wrinkles from a huge, quilted stocking embossed with his name.

"Mama," he said in a voice that said he was thinking about something important.

Amy had moved to the front door where she was busy hanging a snow-flocked wreath. She glanced back over one shoulder. "What, Dexter?"

The boy stopped smoothing, reached into the box and lifted out a fur-lined stocking.

Reed's chest clutched. The stocking bore Ben's name.

"What about Daddy's stocking?"

Amy's eyes widened. Her lips parted in an intake of air. She didn't cry or anything crazy like that, but Reed could tell she'd forgotten about the stocking, wasn't quite prepared to see it, and wasn't sure how to answer her son. This time last year, Ben had been here, hanging his stocking beside theirs, being the dad these boys deserved and the husband Amy needed.

Reed didn't figure anyone could fill the void, least of all him, but he suddenly wanted the James family to have the best Christmas possible.

"I think you should hang it right up there with everyone else's." He glanced at Amy, hoping he hadn't overstepped his bounds.

Her worried expression changed to wonder and then to pleasure in the blink of an eye.

"Reed," she said in a grateful tone that made him gulp. He was no hero. No use in her thinking he was.

Dexter's face lit up. "For real?"

"Sure. Come on, I'll help you find a tack."

"No tacks required, Reed," Amy said. "Use the special mantel holders in the box."

"Oh." How was he supposed to know there were special holders?

"These, Chief." With holders in hand, Dexter scrambled to his feet, eager now. "But what can we put in it? People in Heaven can't eat candy. Can they? Or open presents."

Great. Questions about Heaven. As if he was an expert. He glanced at Amy, who still had that misty-eyed, funny look on her face. She offered no sage bits of advice.

He was on his own—and in over his head.

"Well." Reed rubbed his chin, thinking hard and fast. If he messed this up, Dexter could be scarred for life. "I don't know, Dexter. Maybe they can. But not in the way we do."

Dexter's face screwed up in thought. "How?"

Reed sorted through the handful of Bible stories he knew and came up empty. Stalling for time, he figured out how to attach the holders to the mantel and allowed the boy to hook his father's stocking into place. Then Dexter turned to him, expectant.

"How, Chief?"

Reed went down on one knee beside the boy and his brother, who had come to join them. The slide show of tree lights swept over the pair—blue, green, red and speckled. His pulse drummed in his head, uncertain, awkward, painfully aware that he had no experience with grieving children.

"The way I see it," he said, "people in Heaven don't need things the way we do."

"Mama said Daddy would never be sick or sad ever again."

He ventured a glance toward Amy, who had perched, listening, on the edge of the brick hearth. She nodded, encouraging but silent and pensive.

"I figure your daddy only needs one thing up there in Heaven."

"What is it, Chief?" Dexter's voice was hushed.

"A stocking filled with love from his two favorite people."

Dexter touched an index finger to his chest. "Me and Sammy?"

Reed swallowed. "His two best buddies in the whole world."

"How do we put it in there?"

"Well, let's see. Three smart dudes like us should be able to come up with something." But he couldn't think of a thing. *Come on, Amy. Help a guy out.*

"I know, Chief. We can color Daddy a picture and put it in his stocking. When he looks down from Heaven, he'll see it."

Relief dried the sweat on Reed's forehead. *Thank You, Lord.* "Great idea, Dexter."

"And kisses. Kisses are invisible."

"Every time you think about your dad, you can put a kiss in the stocking."

"Yeah," Dexter breathed, his face lit with happiness at the idea of doing something nice for his daddy. "Thank you, Chief."

And then the innocent little boy went one step further and melted Reed into a puddle of mush. He looped one small hand over Reed's shoulder, looked earnestly into his eyes and said, "Since I can't have Daddy this year, I'm glad we gots you."

Amy thought her heart would burst right out of her chest. Without knowing it, Reed had intuitively given Dexter exactly what he needed.

How could she not care for a man like that?

The thought froze in her brain. Okay, she cared for him. He was a good man. He was amazing with the boys, though sometimes awkward and gruff, but they had figured him out.

Sammy, with his big eyes and baby ways, had the police

chief wrapped around his little finger. And Dexter needed the influence of a strong man.

This was exactly what Ben had been talking about in his letter. He wanted his boys to have a strong father to teach them how to be men. A father to hang stockings and cut down ugly Christmas trees. A father to love them.

She studied the side of Reed's ruggedly handsome face. He was deep in conversation with Dexter, the curve of his mouth and chiseled jawline strong and manly.

She could care for Reed Truscott. Maybe she already did, a suspicion that made her nervous. But what about Reed?

She wanted what was best for her boys, but was it fair to Reed to accept his offer of marriage, simply to give her children a father? Worse, how could she live with a man, knowing he'd married her out of loyalty instead of love?

Amy closed her eyes against the scene being played out in front of the fireplace and did the only thing she could. She prayed.

Chapter Nine

"Cookie cutters in that bottom drawer."

Amy followed the no-nonsense jerk of Granny Crisp's chin and came up with a plastic baggie filled with various Christmas shapes. She'd never imagined Granny as the Christmas cookie type, but apparently the gruff grandmother was a lot like her grandson—tough on the outside, melted caramel inside.

She put the cutters on the table next to Sammy and Dexter, who were making a mess with a roller and sugar cookie dough.

Serious Dexter carefully peeled bits of dough from the roller and patted them back into the pile. Sammy stuck a glob in his mouth. More globs adorned his shirtfront.

Dexter took up a tree cutter. "This one is just like Herbie. I'll make it for Chief Reed. Can we put sprinkles?"

"Sprinkles are up there." Hands deep in dough, Granny offered another chin hitch, this one toward the upper cabinet. "You'll need frosting, too."

She said it as though the notion irritated her, but Amy took her cue from the boys. Granny was just being Granny, gruff and kind all in one feisty package.

"We'll make gingerbread boys for your class at school. You know the story, don't you?"

"What is it, Granny?"

"'Run, run as fast as you can. You can't catch me, I'm the Gingerbread Man!'" Hands aloft and covered with flour, the scrawny woman made a quick dive toward the boys, laughing with glee. Sammy and Dexter giggled and ducked.

Though she'd had her doubts about moving out here until after Christmas, Amy was now glad she had. Mostly. Sammy and Dexter were thriving on the extra attention from Granny and Reed. And she enjoyed the older woman's company. Reed's, too, if she'd admit it. Christmas had taken on a new exuberance, a new radiance since the move. She'd lost the deep dread of facing Christmas without Ben.

"When I was a little girl we made gingerbread men and fancy cookies for all the neighbors and the retirement home," Amy said. "Mom would take me around and let me do the giving. I felt so important."

"Can we do that, Mama?"

"If you don't eat them all first." She pecked a kiss on Dexter's forehead. He smelled like a mixture of sugar, ginger and little boy.

"Reed never had that."

Granny's out-of-context statement turned Amy around. "Never had what? Cookies?"

Granny snorted. "Among other things. His daddy was a hard man. After Shawna died—"

"Reed's mother?"

Granny nodded. "My daughter. She died when Reed was just a pup. Brain tumor. Diagnosed in February, died in May. Just like that, she was gone."

Amy paused, hands on a star-shaped cookie cutter. "How awful for all of you."

"Bad time, that's for sure. If not for the Lord's promise

that she wasn't in pain anymore..." The old woman stopped, cleared her throat and started again. The moisture in her eyes gave away her inner sorrow. "Wes made it worse by whisking my only grandchild off to the Aleutian Islands."

"I can't imagine." And it was true. Losing Ben was hard enough, but if she'd lost her sons as well, the pain would have been too great to bear.

She took Sammy's pudgy hand and helped him cut the star shape, then held her breath while his small fingers carefully moved the limp cookie to the shiny stainless-steel cookie sheet.

"Harder on the boy than me," Granny said, slamming a cabinet door. "I saw him just enough to know how rough his father was on him. Nothing Reed ever did was enough."

Amy aligned Dexter's six Christmas tree shapes in a row on the pan. "Sounds as if Reed's father was mad at the world."

"He was. But Reed suffered for it. No mama or granny to nurture him. No one to bake cookies or read stories."

Amy started to ask why Granny was sharing this with her, but she knew the answer. In her own way, Granny was helping her understand the complex chief of police.

"This is royal frosting. Sets up like a rock." Granny slapped a bowl of frosting on the table. "Having you and those boys here has been good for him. He needs you."

Needed her? Somehow, Amy couldn't see Reed Truscott needing anyone. He was strong and capable, and as dependable as winter in Alaska.

A little voice niggled in her head. She *had* noticed the almost yearning way he'd snuggled next to her boys on the couch while she read to them each evening. The boys were all over him, demanding his attention, and he soaked it up like dry ground. He was sometimes awkward with them, but he tried hard.

Last night, when Sammy had scraped his knee, Reed had

been the go-to guy. Watching the lawman gently clean a scrape on her baby's knee and apply a superhero Band-Aid, all the while telling Sammy that big boys *did* cry if something hurt, had brought a lump to her throat.

It struck her then that Reed's gruffness was not anger. It was not rudeness. Neither was it arrogance. The abrupt, gruff manner was self-protection. He was afraid of being hurt, which shed a new light on the awkward, pushy proposals.

How hard had it been for him to put himself out there, time and again, for her to shoot down?

By the time Reed arrived home from work that night, Amy had returned from a meeting of the town decoration committee and the boys' bedtime was nearing. Sammy and Dexter had rushed to the door and flung themselves at Reed. Amy's heart lifted at the sight, and with Granny's revelations fresh in her mind, she had the strongest urge to join them. For a minute, she considered what it might be like to be held in Reed's arms, against that solid, sturdy, dependable chest.

Instead, she'd followed Granny's instructions, warmed the pot of moose stew and corn bread, and sat at the table making a to-do list, while Reed inhaled a very late dinner. Granny herself had taken a box of cookies and gone to visit a friend.

"Energizer," Reed mumbled around a bite of corn bread.

"What?" she lifted her head from the notepaper.

"Do you ever stop?"

"Too much to do. Especially right now." She scribbled a note to get Sammy's hair cut before the pageant.

"You like doing all this stuff."

She loved it. She loved her town and the people in it. She loved Christmas. She loved feeling useful. She loved life. What reason, other than love, was there to do anything?

"There's a scripture, 'to whom much is given, much is

required,' or something like that. But I don't do things out of duty," she said pointedly. "I do them because I want to."

He finished his stew and got up to put the bowl in the dishwasher. Reed was tidy that way. "Granny trained you well."

"Not just her. My father insisted I pull my own weight. You mess it up, you clean it up."

Was that where he'd developed his overactive sense of responsibility? "Granny told me a little about him today."

He leaned his hips against the cabinet, wary, his face closed. "Yeah?"

She tried a different direction. "It must have been hard losing your mother so young."

He shifted. "Yeah."

"Is that why you're so good with Sammy and Dexter?"

He frowned as though puzzled by the statement. "They're Ben's boys."

Duty again. She was really getting tired of that refrain. Didn't the man do anything from his heart instead of his head? "Ben's boys," as he'd called them, rounded the corner from the hallway, wearing fuzzy, footed pajamas. Sammy's were of a yellow cartoon character and Dexter's were decorated with a red fire engine and a spotted dog. She lifted Sammy onto her lap and hugged Dexter against her side.

"You smell good," she said, giving a giant sniff against Sammy's neck. "Did you brush your teeth?"

"Uh-huh." He flashed a fake smile. "See."

"Me, too." Dexter offered his own fake smile. "All ready for bed." He opened his mouth in a giant yawn. "I'm sleepy."

"Okay. You two go on up and I'll be there in a few minutes, after I finish this list and call Casey. She's starting a new tour in the morning. I want to be sure everything is set."

She pushed back from the table just as Reed pushed away from the countertop and lifted a palm. "You stay put. Do what you need to do. I'll put the boys to bed."

Dexter flung himself onto Reed's knees. "You will? Will you read us a story, too? Please."

She could see Reed hadn't bargained on that.

"Well." He rubbed a hand over the back of his neck. "You sure you don't want to wait on your mom? She's good at that kind of thing."

Amy laughed. "Coward. It's a picture book. You can do it."

Reed figured there was a first time for everything. A week or so ago, he'd listened to his first bedtime story. At least the first one he could remember. And now he was reading one.

He sat on the edge of the double bed, in one of his guest rooms, where both little boys had taken up residence. No one had ever stayed here, and now he couldn't think of this as anyone's room but Sammy and Dexter's. Funny how the two little dudes had wiggled their way into the fabric of his life, and he dreaded the day they'd move out again.

So far, their mother seemed no closer to accepting his proposal than she ever had. He'd failed Ben in that way, but he was trying hard not to fail him with the boys. Ben had probably read to them every night, using funny voices. Ben had probably been great at story time.

Sammy looped a tiny hand around Reed's elbow and gazed up at him with a sweet expression. "We're ready, Chief."

Reed cleared his throat. "Right." He opened the oversize hardback book and began to read. They seemed to be on a Christmas story kick.

Another hand, slightly larger, snaked around from the opposite side to claim his other elbow and his heart. He could smell the clean soap and toothpaste scent of them and feel their warmth spreading through him. Occasionally as he read, they'd wiggle closer. Finally, Dexter sat up in bed and leaned his head on Reed's shoulder with a deep sigh.

He'd never felt this way before. Domesticated. Warm. Settled. At home in his own house. He draped an arm around Dexter's shoulders and snuggled him close. Maybe Amy was right. He felt sorry for Ben's boys because he understood losing a parent at an early age.

No, it was more than that. He was getting attached. The thought troubled him. What if he let them down? What if he hurt them in some way without meaning to?

"Chief Weed," Sammy said when the book ended.

"What, buddy?"

"We gotta say our prayers."

He'd gone out on a limb again and cut himself off. He knew half of the Lord's Prayer. Was that enough?

The little boy wiggled from beneath the covers and dropped to his knees beside the bed. His brother followed.

"Come on, Chief."

Feeling as helpless as a beached whale, Reed slipped to his knees between the children. Not knowing what else to do, he draped an arm over each child.

Hands clasped and eyes shut tight, Dexter led off with Sammy doing a tag-team prayer of thank-yous and God blesses.

Their heartfelt, endearing conversation with God made Reed realize how little he understood about being God's child. Maybe it was time he started finding out.

Halfway through the prayer, the hair rose on the back of his neck and he knew Amy had come upstairs. He could feel her there at the door, listening in. Every nerve in his body responded whenever she moved inside his radar. She was getting under his skin something fierce. Not just because of the spot Ben had put them both in, not because of the treasure or the danger—but because Amy was the most amazing woman he'd ever known—warm and funny and loving.

He was afraid his foolish heart had gotten attached to more

than the little boys. But Amy would never think of him that way. She'd said so herself. No one could take Ben's place.

He sighed heavily.

Doing the right thing had quickly become doing the hard thing—something he thought he was used to. How did he keep his promise to Ben without getting his heart trampled?

Chapter Ten

Reed stomped the snow and mush off his boots as he stepped from the sidewalk into the General Store. Cy, knowing he was welcome in the establishment, came too, flicking bits of brown moisture onto the ancient green tile.

"Morning, Chief."

"Morning, Doc." Reed nodded at Dr. Alex Havens, who was leaving as Reed entered.

"Old Harry's in one of his moods this morning. Look out."

Reed snorted and went on inside. Harry was often in a snit. If he let Harry's surliness keep him away, he'd never buy supplies.

He entered to find the store quieter than usual, without the normal chatter of three or four older gents around the stove in back.

"Where's the spit-and-whittle club?" He aimed his question at the pot-bellied store owner, grinning a little at the nickname he'd given the old men who loitered in the general store for company and conversation.

"Don't know. Don't care." Harry slumped morosely against the counter. "What do you need, Chief?"

Harry wasn't the friendliest guy in town, but he usually

wasn't this cranky. Something was up. "Who put coal in your stocking?"

"Me, I guess. I'm an old fool."

"That right?" Reed wasn't one to pry into personal business, but he'd known Harry since the day he arrived in Treasure Creek. For all his outward grouchiness, Harry was a fine man. Reed had delivered more than one sack of groceries anonymously to someone down on his luck—groceries paid for by Harry Peterson. He'd also known the businessman to extend credit to someone he knew might never repay. "What's up?"

"Women."

Tell me about it, he wanted to say. He was having fits with the feelings Amy James had stirred up inside him. Not wanting to share that little tidbit of trouble, he ambled toward the coffeepot Harry kept bubbling behind the counter and poured himself a cup he didn't really want. "All women? Or someone particular?"

"Yeah. That."

Reed spooned sugar into the cup and sipped. He could always count on Harry to make good coffee. "Joleen Jones?"

"Yeah. Her."

"I thought you weren't interested."

"'Course I was. Am." Harry slammed a wet cloth against the counter. "What kind of idiot wouldn't be interested in a fine woman like Joleen?"

Reed kept a poker face. Lots of men in Treasure Creek found Joleen's high-pressure antics a little too strong, even Harry for a while. "What changed your mind? Neville Weeks?"

"Why would she go out with a scrawny stick of a man like him?" Harry scrubbed the wet rag over the counter, rubbing hard enough to remove the fading speckled design.

"Is she going out with Neville? You know this for a fact?"

"I was standing in the door." Harry pointed. The cloth dangled from his right hand, bleach scent thick. "Right over there. Joleen came prancing by with Neville trailing her like a hound dog. And you know what?"

"What?"

"She never so much as said hello to me." He slapped the rag back onto the counter.

Reed shook his head, sympathetic but amused. "Women."

"Exactly."

Reed set his coffee mug on the counter, careful to avoid Harry's scrubbing cloth, and leaned on an elbow. "Face it, Harry. You weren't exactly encouraging to Joleen. Maybe she gave up on you."

Harry paused in midscrub, his jaw sagging. "A man can change."

"Well then, do it."

"What? Change? How? What can I do to win her over? Tell me, Chief, and I'll give it a try."

"Me? How would I know?" Considering how badly he was doing in that department himself, Reed found it hilarious as well as ironic for Harry to be asking him for relationship advice. For days he'd pondered what to do about Amy. Being with her was eating a hole inside him, a hole that she was filling with her joyful smile and funny socks and nurturing ways.

"I want her back. Not that I ever had her in the first place, but you know what I mean."

He did. Joleen had made no secret of her attraction to the store owner.

"Well..." Reed rubbed his fingertips over the countertop worn smooth by time and enterprise. "I'm no expert, but I figure all women like to be wined and dined. Least, that's what I've always heard."

Harry drew away, appalled. "I'm not a drinking man. You know that."

"It's just an expression, Harry. Take Joleen someplace nice and show her a good time. You could even buy her some flowers or candy or something. All women like flowers, don't they?" Maybe he should ask Amy about that? Did Amy like flowers?

Annoyed that his brain seemed stuck on a certain little redhead, he ground his back teeth.

"Flowers? Sure, sure. Great idea." Harry's depressed face had changed to animation. "What kind do you think she'd like?"

Was there more than one kind? "Roses."

"In Alaska in December?"

Reed shrugged. "You order supplies in from the Lower 48 all the time. Why not roses?"

He wondered if Amy liked roses.

"I can do it. You're right. If I can't get 'em, maybe that wedding place down the street can. I recollect roses at Mattie Starks's funeral last month." Harry reached across the counter and clapped Reed on the shoulders. "I can't thank you enough, Chief."

"Don't thank me yet. She might be allergic."

Harry's face fell. "You think?"

"I was joking, Harry. Order the roses. Call Martelli's Restaurant and make a reservation. Then call Joleen and invite her out for the time of her life. Show her your natural charm. Show her she's special. A woman needs that."

His words pierced his own heart. A woman needs to know she's special. Amy was special. Had he ever told her that? Of course not. She was Ben's wife.

He gulped. Not wife. *Widow.* A widow he not only liked a lot, but one he found attractive in every sense of the term.

Should he feel guilty about thinking such a thing? Was he being disloyal to Ben? Would Amy pack her bags and leave if he even hinted at the emotional turmoil she was causing?

Maybe. Then again, maybe not. Amy hadn't gone snowmobiling with Ethan Eckles, or anywhere else with him for that matter. But she might the next time the piano player telephoned. She was young and pretty and alone. She wouldn't stay single forever.

"Harry?"

"Yeah?"

"When you order those roses?"

"Yeah?"

"Order an extra dozen."

Amy slid on a pair of sparkling earrings and turned her head to look in the mirror. Her cheeks were flushed and her eyes glowed with the excitement stirring inside her. For some reason, Reed had asked her to dinner at Martelli's, the nicest restaurant in town.

At first she'd been too shocked to answer, but when he cleared his throat and said, "Maybe you don't want to. That's okay," Amy had remembered how difficult it was for Reed Truscott to express his feelings. He was asking her for a date. A real date. And she not only didn't want to hurt his feelings, she wanted to go. With Reed. On a date. Without her sons.

The realization was a direct hit to her good sense.

Granny Crisp, of course, the matchmaking little sourdough, had harrumphed, eyes sparkling, and announced her intention to spend the evening making a gingerbread house with Dexter and Sammy. Reed and Amy would just have to go by themselves. Reed had laughed so hard at the obvious ploy that

Granny spun on her heel and marched off, muttering under her breath.

Amy drew a brush through her hair one last time, added a dab of shiny pink gloss to her lips and stood back to check her appearance. She would do. Granted, an emerald-green sweater dress with heavy black leggings and knee-high boots was as fancy as she dared get in this weather. Should she wear that long, silver necklace? The one that reached her waist?

"Maybe the matching bracelets, too." She added the seldom worn jewelry.

Down below, the doorbell peeled.

She took another glance in the long mirror and then sighed. "Stop fussing, Amy," she muttered. "It's probably not a real date anyway."

Would she be disappointed if it wasn't? What if he tried another of his pushy proposals? She groaned. Why hadn't she thought of that when he first asked?

The doorbell rang again. Where were Granny Crisp and Reed?

Oh, well, she was ready. She'd get it.

Jogging down the staircase, she went to the front door where she could see the outline of a figure through the peep-hole. A familiar female figure holding a large bouquet of flowers.

Bewildered, she flung the door wide, letting in a blast of frigid air. "Bethany, hi. Are you lost?"

Her friend, Bethany, grinned from inside the hood of a fur-lined parka. "Nope. These are for you. Take them before they freeze."

"For me?"

"That's what the card says." Bethany's grin widened, growing speculative. "We wondered when this might happen."

"When what might happen?"

"You. Chief Truscott. Living out here together." Bethany

shrugged. "Not that we didn't understand, mind you, what with the break-in and all. It just seems natural."

Casey had warned her that speculation was rife, but she'd laughed it off. "These are from Reed?"

"You expecting roses from someone else?"

"Bethany, stop it. Reed and I are good friends. Have been for years. You know that."

All right, so maybe they were moving toward being more than friends. She just wasn't sure yet, and she certainly wasn't ready to be the object of gossip.

"You must be freezing. Want to come inside and warm up? I can make some hot cider."

Bethany shook her head and backed away. "Looks like you're getting ready to go somewhere. The truck is warm, and I have to get back to the shop. I'll see you at the tree lighting?"

"Oh, sure. I'll be there."

"With the chief?"

"Bethany!" Amy said in exasperation.

Bethany laughed and left the porch with a backward wave.

Dazed, Amy shut the door and carried the unexpected flowers into the kitchen. Outside, she heard the wedding planner's four-wheel drive grind down the incline toward the main road. Reed's heavy footsteps turned her around.

"Did you send these?" she demanded. Of course, he had. It said so right there on the card.

He stopped dead still, guilty as charged, his eyes shifting from one side to the other. "You hate roses?"

A confused mix of tears and laughter bubbled in her throat. No one, not even Ben, had ever sent her roses. "I love them."

"Then why are you mad?"

"I..." She stuck her nose in the flowers and breathed in.

"I'm not mad. I'm stunned and…" She blinked back unwelcome tears. "Thank you. This is the nicest surprise I've ever had."

His whole demeanor changed. "Seriously?"

"Yes." Ben had been a good husband, but he'd never been one for romantic gifts or flowers. Amy hadn't thought she was, either, until now, when her heart felt so full she could hardly breathe.

"Well." Reed nodded. "You look…nice."

"So do you." And she was not joking. Reed, out of uniform for once, wore black wool slacks and a red sweater over a white shirt and dark tie. Over all this he'd added a gray blazer. Who knew he had such great taste in clothes?

"Your coat, madam?" he said, holding out her heavy parka.

Amy made a face. "Wish I had a fancy mink to wear."

She slid her arms into the jacket. Reed slipped the parka up onto her shoulders and let his hands linger there. "You have beautiful hair."

The statement was so out of character for reticent Reed that Amy was dumbstruck. Slowly, she turned and smiled up at the tall lawman standing inches away. With a hitch in her throat and a song in her heart, she breathed in his warm, woodsy aftershave and allowed him to guide her out the door and into his vehicle.

Amy had ridden with Reed many times, but tonight felt like the first time, as she saw him in a new light. This was not Reed the hard-eyed, demanding cop, but Reed the gentleman. A little tentative and shy at first, as if they were teenagers on a first date, but solicitous and respectful, asking her opinion, complimenting her dress and her hair. Amy's nerve endings buzzed with energy.

When they reached Martelli's Restaurant, she reached for

her door handle only to have strong fingers stop her. "My job. The lady sits tight."

He hopped out of the SUV and rounded the front, head down against the wind. She watched his journey with an eagerness she'd forgotten—the eagerness of a woman attracted to a man, waiting to be in his company again.

He opened her door and took her hand, helping her out. The snow in the parking area was packed and slick. "Careful. Hold on."

He tucked her hand into his bent elbow and led the way. Amy's pulse skittered along with her feet.

Was she ready for this?

Martelli's Restaurant was by far the most elegant place in all of Treasure Creek. Leaving the frigid air outside, Reed guided Amy into the warm, inviting establishment, where they were greeted by a hostess.

"Chief Truscott, your table is ready. This way, please."

He exchanged amused glances with Amy. Both of them knew the young woman, as they did almost everyone in town, but tonight her warm smile was polite and professional, in keeping with the more upscale dining atmosphere of the restaurant.

With a hand riding lightly at Amy's back, Reed followed the hostess to a corner table, where she placed two menus across from each other. Soft candlelight illuminated white linens and fan-folded napkins, heavy silver utensils and gleaming stemware. No moose antlers or animal heads hanging from the walls, and not a plaid flannel shirt in sight.

Was he ever out of his element!

"I haven't been here in a long time," Amy said as she settled into her spindle-backed chair.

"Make that two of us," he said, gazing around at the quiet, cozy, intimate dining room. "I hope you like it."

"Coming here is a nice change of pace from pizza with the boys or lunch at Lizbet's."

"Or stew with Granny?"

Amy laughed, exactly the effect he'd been hoping for. Nothing lifted his spirits like Amy's all-out laugh. All decked out in a green dress that set her hair on fire, the woman took his breath away. In fact, his chest was tight enough to burst.

"This is really nice, Reed. And I love the roses. That was such a sweet thing to do." She reached across the table and placed her hand atop his. His heart bumped his rib cage.

"I wish—"

The waitress arrived to take their order and Amy sat back, whatever she was about to say was lost. Disappointment filtered over him. What exactly did Amy wish? And what did it have to do with his invitation and gift of roses? Dare he ask?

"Filet mignon," he said to the waitress. "Two."

Amy lifted an eyebrow but didn't argue. When the waitress left, he explained. "I figured you wouldn't order it otherwise."

"You were right. I wouldn't have."

"Why? You don't like filet mignon?"

She leaned forward, blue eyes dancing, and whispered, "It's expensive."

His heart did that crazy leaping thing again, and he was sorely tempted to touch her face. She was right there, inches away. All he'd have to do is lift his hand from the table and cup her chin. Then he'd know if her skin was as silky as he suspected. The room was dim and no one was looking. Maybe he'd even kiss her.

"Sir, would you like to see our wine list?" The waitress had reappeared from nowhere.

Reed sat back, startled by his wayward thoughts. When had he begun thinking of Amy as kissable? She was Ben's widow, and for a second he hated that painful truth worse than he hated his part in Ben's untimely death.

"No wine, thank you," he heard Amy say. "But I'd love a cappuccino. What about you, Reed?"

"Sure."

He'd never had a cappuccino in his life. In fact, he'd never be in a situation like this before, when he wanted so much and felt so helpless. Taking care of Amy was a promise he'd made, but he didn't just want her to be protected and provided for. He wanted her to be happy, to have nice things like steak and cappuccino, and enough money so she didn't have to worry about the town or her business. He wondered what Ben would think of that.

The waitress brought their drinks and they both sipped, saying nothing more for a few minutes. The silence was comfortable, like two old friends would be, but different, too. Reed wished he was a sparkling conversationalist, able to impress Amy in some way. But he was just himself. A small-town police chief with more flaws than the Yukon had fish.

"Amy! Chief Truscott! Yoo-hoo."

The high-pitched, Southern voice could belong to no one but Joleen Jones. Reed laid his fork aside and turned toward the sound, just as the fluffy bleached blonde approached their table.

"Don't you two look cute together?" Joleen gushed a hiccoughing giggle and pressed three fingers to her lips. "I'd heard the rumors, but now I know it's true. I'm so happy for you."

Reed watched as Amy glanced down, a flush cresting her cheekbones. This silly woman had embarrassed her.

"We're having dinner," he said, hoping his frown would defray any further speculation.

"Us, too." Joleen giggled again and fluttered a wave toward an approaching man. "Isn't he the handsomest thing?"

Harry Peterson, pot belly and all, came into view. When he spotted Reed, his usual frown was replaced by a grin. "Joleen said she spotted the pair of you over here. Place is so dark I couldn't see much of anything."

Fluttering her eyelashes like crazy, Joleen latched on to Harry's arm and leaned against his shoulder. "But romantic, too. I love sitting in the dark with you, Harry."

Harry's chest puffed out and he patted her hand. "Anything for the prettiest girl in town."

"Oh, Harry, you say the sweetest things. Doesn't he say the sweetest things?" she asked Amy.

Amy smiled. She must be as amused by the pair as Reed was, but her response was kind. "I can see you're having a good time."

"We are. Now, if you will excuse us, we'll just mosey back over into that cozy little corner by the fireplace. Are you ready, Harry?"

"When you are, darlin'."

"Nice seeing you here, Amy. You two, Chief. Toodle-oo for now." Joleen hunched her shoulders and giggled up at Harry, who beamed in response.

As the pair walked away, Harry glanced back, winked and lifted his hand in a thumbs-up.

The waitress came with their steaks, refilled their water glasses and departed again. Reed waited, knowing Amy would pray whether they were in public or not. When she bowed her head, he did likewise and was pleasantly surprised to find himself full of gratitude to a God he'd seldom acknowledged. He credited Amy's influence with the change. She made him aware of how good his life was, something he'd never taken time to consider.

When the prayer ended, Amy looked up with a smile. "The steak smells incredible. I could hardly pray for inhaling."

He chuckled. "Same here. This loaded baked potato's calling my name, too."

Daintily slicing into her filet, Amy said, "Joleen and Harry are certainly an unlikely pair."

"You can say that again."

"Love is funny that way."

Fork and knife aloft, Reed's heart jumped. "Meaning?"

"You and I might see an overzealous Southern woman with big hair and a grumpy middle-aged man with a spare tire around his middle. Love sees with the heart."

"You think they're in love?"

"They both looked happier together than I've ever seen either of them look apart." She took a roll from the basket and dabbed it lightly with butter. "If they aren't in love now, they soon will be."

"Are you a romantic, too?"

"I never thought of myself as one, but maybe I am." She cocked her head to one side, grinning. "Maybe the roses did it."

Did that mean she was feeling romantic about him? Or just romantic in general?

"I should have ordered roses before."

"Why, Reed," she said, fluttering her lashes in a cute imitation of Joleen. "You say the sweetest things."

They both laughed.

"Be careful with those fancy eyelashes. I might lure you into that dark corner Joleen mentioned."

She fluttered them again and Reed was almost positive she was flirting. With him.

And he liked it.

Chapter Eleven

Amy didn't know what had gotten into her tonight. Something about the romantic atmosphere of Martelli's, the endearing courtship of Joleen and Harry, and most of all, Reed's company had brought out the woman in her. She'd laughed and flirted and thoroughly enjoyed the attentions of an attractive man. Reed, too, seemed to have enjoyed himself tonight. They'd avoided hot-button topics like the treasure and Ben's death, and she'd watched the staid cop blossom into a charming date.

Now, as they rode back to Reed's ranch house, she glanced at his profile, angular and strong in the semidarkness of the vehicle.

"What?" he said, his mouth curving into a smile. "You want to go somewhere else? Maybe scrounge up a banana split or a piece of hot apple pie?"

"Too full of good steak for that. We'd better go home." She patted her overfilled tummy. Though she wouldn't mind extending their evening, they both had work tomorrow. "As Dorothy would tell you, there's no place like home—and morning comes early for both of us."

He glanced her way. "Thanks."

"For what?" she asked.

"For thinking of my place as home."

She tilted her head, reading the meaning behind the statement. Reed needed to be needed. "The boys love being there."

"What about their mom?"

"Her, too," she answered honestly. As strange as it seemed, she and her sons had settled into Reed's home as if they belonged there. A sense of security such as she hadn't known in over a year resided inside the walls of Reed's ranch. But it wasn't only the feeling of protection. It was Reed himself.

She was attracted to Reed. More than attracted. And Amy wasn't quite sure what to do with the feelings.

Reed reached across the seat and found her hand. Funny how something as junior-high as clasping hands made her pulse tremble and her heart sing. She looked across at him and smiled. Even in the dim light of the dashboard, she saw him smile in return.

A peaceful contentment settled over the warm, cozy cab, as they drove the rest of the way home in silence, holding hands.

When they arrived at the ranch, the house was dark and quiet, except for a light left on in the garage. Reed parked the car and got out, coming around to open her door. He took her hand again and they went inside.

Amy reached for the light beside the kitchen door, but Reed's hand stopped her. "Wait."

She tilted toward him, puzzled. "Why?"

His hands drifted to her waist and he held her lightly. "Thank you for tonight."

Amy smiled. "I had a great time."

"Me, too. The best in..." He laughed softly, pensively. "Forever, I guess."

Amy found the admission endearing.

"Better than our Christmas tree outing?" she asked, trying for a lighter note.

"Not better, but different. Just you and me. Alone."

Oh. Her pulse bumped.

Toenails tapping on vinyl announced Cy's entrance. He grazed her legs, then greeted Reed with a gentle butt of his massive head. Neither paid the dog any mind.

"Can I tell you something?" Reed asked, the rumble of his voice quiet.

"We've been friends forever. You can tell me anything."

He took a half step closer. She could see him clearly, though the room was illuminated only by the digital clocks and the glow of firelight and the lit-up Christmas tree seeping in from the living room. "I've been thinking."

Amy considered a silly retort about Christmas gifts or the danger of thinking, but something in Reed's tone stopped her. "About?"

"Maybe I don't want to be friends anymore."

All the air rushed out of her lungs.

"I..." She opened her mouth to ask what he meant, but the answer was in the way his head lowered and his eyes fluttered shut. He was going to kiss her. And she was going to let him.

The kiss was sweet and tender and questioning. A warm, brief whisper of a kiss that set Amy's head to reeling. A paradigm shift occurred somewhere in the back of her brain. Reed Truscott was more than a friend. A lot more.

She pulled away, unsure of what she wanted from Reed and even more unsure of what he wanted from her.

That was the question that bothered her most. Could Reed be falling for her? Or would his promise to Ben always come between them?

* * *

Reed watched Amy scurry up the stairs without looking back, the silver chain around her neck clicking lightly as she ran.

With a deep sigh, he rubbed a hand over his face. "Blew it again, Truscott."

He shouldn't be surprised, considering how little he knew about the kind of man a woman wanted. He knew how to be a cop. He knew how to wrangle a budget, run an office. He knew how to run a fishing boat and how to build a house with his bare hands. But he could put what he knew about being a family man on the tip of a pencil.

Perhaps he'd offended Amy with the kiss. Maybe he'd moved too fast, been too pushy. She claimed he was good at that.

Suddenly, cold to the heart, he went into the living room and banked the fireplace. Then he pulled his old recliner close to the flames and extended his sock-covered feet. Plain, ordinary thermal socks. Not zany, happy socks like Amy's. Tonight she'd worn a pair of electric knee-highs, warmed by a tiny battery attached to the tall top. He'd laughed when she showed him.

Shoot, he'd laughed at every cute thing she said.

Sighing again, he stared into the flames and remembered the too-short kiss. He should have asked permission, he supposed, but he'd acted before his brain had engaged. And when he tasted her sweet mouth, his brain had shorted out. He'd have gone on kissing her if she hadn't pulled away.

What would Ben think of him tonight? Would he punch his lights out? Or cheer him on? Had Ben expected him to court Amy, maybe even fall in love with her? What had he meant that day when they'd trekked through the wilderness and he'd asked Reed to take care of Amy and the boys if anything should happen to him?

"Marry her, Reed. Be a father to my boys."

At first, Reed had laughed him off, sure that nothing would ever happen to an invincible wilderness expert like Ben. But in the end, he'd promised. And that promise haunted him still, a vow made to a dead man.

"I'm trying, buddy," he whispered to the crackling fire, where it seemed he could see Ben's eyes peering out at him.

His dog, stretched full length on the rug beside the hearth, opened his one good eye, then closed it again.

Reed ran a weary hand over the back of his neck. He'd never be the man Ben James had been. He figured Amy thought the same.

Sunday morning, Reed's quick, questioning kiss lingered in Amy's mind like the sweet smell of roses lingered over the kitchen table. Awash in confusion, she'd rushed up the stairs and away from temptation. Part of her knew this was what Ben had wanted. But what about what Reed wanted—really wanted deep down in his heart. Was the date, the roses, the gentle kiss, for himself? Or out of loyalty to Ben?

She didn't know. And until she did, she'd have to hold her emotions in check—not an easy task for Amy James.

But today was the Lord's day, and Amy loved Sunday mornings—a time to give all her emotion and attention to her Savior and Friend. This was the next-to-last Sunday before the pageant, a fact that gave her the jitters. She wanted everything to be perfect.

"Are you boys ready for breakfast?" she called as she bounded down the stairs toward the kitchen.

A snicker, followed by a *shh* was her first clue that her two menaces were up to something.

"Boys?" With amused concern, she rounded the doorway into the kitchen and stopped at the sight before her. "What are you up to?"

With Dexter and Sammy, the sky was the limit, but if they messed up Granny's kitchen, she'd have their hides. The smell of food, especially bacon, however, made her stomach growl.

Both boys and Reed spun around, blocking the view of the table. All three were dressed and ready for church—including Reed, a stunning accomplishment in itself, and all three wore secretive smiles.

"Where's Granny?" she asked, suspicious.

"I'm right behind you." The wiry woman cycloned in, still attired in a heavy robe and slippers, to point a skinny finger at her grandson. "What's going on in my kitchen?"

Uh-oh. This better be good.

Reed glanced at Dexter and Sammy and nodded. The three parted like the Red Sea, to reveal a table laden with pancakes, bacon, juice and coffee. "Breakfast is ready."

Sammy bounced up and down, clapping. "Surprise, Mommy. Surprise, Granny. Me and Dexter and Chief Weed made breakfast. Do you love it?"

Happiness bubbled up inside Amy. She swept the baby-faced child into her arms for a hug. "Yes. And come here, you," she said to Dexter.

He fell against her giggling. "Hug Chief Reed. He helped, too."

The kitchen suddenly felt too warm. Before the dinner date, she would have hugged Reed and laughed. But now things were different. She'd relived that kiss a thousand times, and now every time she looked at him her heart jumped. She wanted to ask if his kiss had meant anything, if *she* meant anything more than obligation, but she was afraid of the answer. Either way had its drawbacks.

The uncomfortable moment passed when Reed pulled out a chair. "Come on, everyone. We don't want to be late for church."

"We?" Amy asked as she settled at the table between Dexter and Sammy.

"I'm going."

And to the delight of everyone, he did.

Redemption Christian Church was a catchall fellowship for almost everyone in town. The pretty country church, complete with a sky-high, pointed steeple, stood at the end of the main thoroughfare where it had been built a hundred years before as the town's focal point. Careful tending kept the old church as beautiful as ever.

Reed's eyes roamed over the congregation, a mismatched group of old-timers, newcomers and folks coming down out of the wilderness to worship. They dressed as they lived: some in suits and ties, others in flannel and mukluks. And Reed figured it was a testament to their honest faith that the wealthy sat with the poor, the hermit with the business owner.

The service started with songs from a hymnal, and if Reed noticed Ethan Eckles glancing at Amy, he couldn't help it. After the music came announcements about the pageant and next Saturday's tree lighting, and finally the preacher took the pulpit.

Though Reed had spent little time here, or in any church for that matter, and figured he was twenty-some years late in starting a relationship with God, the preacher's message seemed right on time. He'd been doing some reading, and a lot of listening to Amy and Pastor Ed and the others during pageant practice. A man needed God whether he wanted to admit it or not. Reed Truscott needed God. What better time than Christmas to make a new start in the right direction?

"Jesus came to earth without fanfare, except to those few shepherds out in the fields," Pastor Ed was saying. "He made no demands, no fuss, though He was the King of Kings come down from Heaven. He made that sacrifice for one reason.

Love for all mankind. A love so great we can't comprehend it. It's a gift that cost Him everything, but it costs you nothing. All you have to do is accept."

Reed squeezed his eyes shut and listened to the choir singing "Love Came Down." The pastor was right. All he had to do was accept.

Jesus, his heart whispered. *If You'll have me, here I am. Warts and all. Help me be the man I should be, the man my father wasn't.*

At the thought of his father, bitterness rose in his chest like a weed springing up to choke out the flower of renewed faith. A quiet battle ensued. He could let his bitterness take control or he could let it go. The choice was his to make, and so he made it, mentally watching the bitter weed wither and die as the flower flourished.

When he opened his eyes, the world was the same, but different. He turned to share the moment with Amy and saw moisture in her eyes. She knew. Without a word, she embraced him, and he felt like a brand-new man.

After church Amy was surrounded by friends discussing the pageant, the Christmas tree lighting next Saturday and the treasure. By association, Reed was swept into the happy melee. The sun, which had decided to shine this particular Sunday, beamed a blinding light off the mounds of snow piled along the streets and covering the ground. The snowplow had done its job with its usual efficiency, though clearing streets was a never-ending process in Alaska's winter.

The sky was clear and the temperature was just below freezing, balmy weather for native Alaskans. Puffs of vapor swirled around smiling faces. Reed, with hands in his pockets and shoulders hunched against the cold, figured he'd remember this day and this peaceful feeling for as long as he lived.

With laughter and waves, the assembly gradually drifted apart. Car doors slammed and motors chugged off to Crock-Pot dinners or lunch at Lizbet's.

Pastor Ed broke away from the last compliment to his sermon and came toward Reed with an extended hand. "Brought you something."

Reed took the small booklet. "What's this?"

"Amy told me you accepted the Lord during invitation. This is a Christianity 101 booklet."

"Christianity for dummies?" Reed asked, but he tendered the question with a smile.

Pastor Ed laughed and clapped Reed on the shoulder. "If you need to talk, have any questions, anything, give me a call. Let me pretend I'm useful."

Emotion clogged Reed's throat. He cleared it. "Thank you, Pastor. I'll do that."

The men shook hands and Pastor Ed headed back into the church with a parting reminder about the final pageant practices in the coming week.

Amy, full of her usual energy, jitterbugged around him. "Let's celebrate. I'll buy you dinner."

"What are we celebrating, Mama?" Dexter asked.

"Reed and Jesus are best friends forever."

"Cool. Can I have a hot dog?"

Both adults laughed. Reed scuffed an open hand across Dexter's hair. "Tell you what—I think Granny has something in the oven for Sunday dinner. Let's go home to eat so she doesn't skin us alive, then I'll take you sledding."

Dexter began to hop up and down, shouting, "Sledding."

Sammy, not to be outdone, followed suit. After a few jumps and shouts, he tugged Reed's coat. "What's sledding?"

Reed scooped Sammy into his arms and headed toward the car. "I'll show you, little man. We'll have fun."

* * *

By the time they arrived home, all four of them were excited about the prospect of an afternoon of sledding. They ate quickly and Amy gathered appropriate clothing and gear while Reed scrounged around in the storage building for two old sleds he'd never used.

"The former police chief left them," he told Amy as he dragged the sleds into the garage and checked to determine if the wooden structures were sound.

"He raised five kids," she said. "Sleds were a necessity."

Reed hadn't known the former chief, whose death had precipitated Reed's hiring, but from the evidence left behind, his had been an active, outdoors family. He'd been glad to buy the other man's ranch when the widow decided to leave everything and move to Oregon to be near her now-grown daughters. It had been simple and easy at the time, and he'd even had thoughts of a family of his own someday. Maybe he was having those thoughts again.

"I saw a couple of bikes in there, too. When the boys get big enough, I'll fix them up and..." He bit down on his back teeth and clamped tight.

What was the matter with him anyway, talking as if Amy and the boys were permanent residents?

"I just meant..." He shrugged, helpless. He didn't know what he meant—a real good reason to keep his mouth shut.

Amy took pity on him. She put a hand on his arm. "Ben would appreciate all you've done for us."

Reed gave one short nod and reached for a rope that he tied securely onto the front of the sled. For once, Ben had been the furthest person from his mind, but apparently not from Amy's.

By the time the sleds were waxed and oiled and considered hill-worthy, the natural exuberance of Amy and her sons had erased the discomfort of sticking his foot in his mouth. Today was special and they were going to have fun.

Off they trudged through the thick snow to the steep incline surrounding his yard.

"This is the hill." Reed stopped and pointed down a long, gentle slope. "It should be smooth and easy to navigate. Fast enough to be fun for us. Slow enough to be safe for the boys."

"And it doesn't lead to a road."

"I don't get much traffic out here."

"Still…"

"Right. No roads." He turned toward the boys, riding happily on the sleds being pulled by the adults. "Hear that, Dexter and Sammy? Safety first. Never sled toward a road."

"Okay." Both boys listened with unusual attentiveness.

"If the sled ever goes too fast or gets out of control, you should roll off into the snow."

"How?"

"Like this." He demonstrated a slow sideways topple and roll. "It's fun. Try it."

They did. "Come on, Mama. Try it."

Amy rolled, too, and then offered to pull each of them on the sled so they could try a roll from a moving sled.

"I'll pull Dexter. You pull Sammy."

With giggles and squeals, and Amy and Reed huffing and puffing through the snow like Clydesdales, each boy rolled from his sled over and over again, until finally Dexter said, "Can we go faster now?"

Reed turned to Amy. "What do you say, Mom? Can they go faster now?"

Amy pretended to consider. "They've been good boys today. And it is almost Christmas, when special things happen for good little boys."

"Big boys, too," he said.

"Oh, but have you been good?"

He grinned wickedly and hopped onto the sled behind Dexter. "We're about to find out."

They whizzed down the hill and Dexter's gleeful laugh touched a spot inside Reed. He found himself laughing because the child was laughing. Before long he was laughing and shouting just for the joy of living. Voices rang out through the woods and echoed back a dozen times.

They sailed past snow-kissed evergreens and snowdrifts over their heads. Winter birds, stunned by the unexpected disturbance, fluttered in the trees, sending cascades of powdery snow drifting to the trail. The deep green forest was rich with winter life, blinding white snow, and the scent of clean, crisp mountain air.

Each run became another. They trudged back up the hill, dragging the sleds and most often the kids. Reed had trouble paying attention to anything except Amy's face, animated as it was by cold, exercise and delight. Her red hair peeked out from under a beige knit hat, a bright contrast to their white surroundings, and her eyes were bluer than the stunning, clear sky. She hopped up and down, clapping with the same enthusiasm as her children.

At one point, as they gathered the sleds and started the walk uphill, Reed hoisted the short-legged Sammy onto his shoulders. Sammy wrapped his thickly mittened hands around Reed's neck and squeezed.

"Chief Weed," he said, leaning down against Reed's ear. "You know what?"

"What, buddy?"

"I love you."

Something incredible and healing shifted beneath Reed's breastbone. With one hand dragging the sled rope and the other holding the child's leg, all he could do was give Sammy a little knee pat. But he was choked up, amazed, thrilled. Maybe it was possible after all. Maybe he could do this fatherhood thing for Ben. No, not for Ben. For Sammy and Dexter. He looked across at the woman trudging along beside him. Nose red as Rudolph's, she grinned at him. For Amy, too. And himself. He didn't have to be like his father.

Feeling lighthearted, he reached the top of the hill and settled Sammy into his spot at the front of the sled. "We'll race you," he told Amy.

Amy pointed at him. "You're on, dude."

At her signal, they pushed off, running hard for several feet before leaping onto the sled. The wind whipped Reed's face and blew his toboggan cap askew. The sleds ran side-by-side for a while, and teasing insults flew back and forth.

"What's the matter, Officer? Can't you beat a girl?"

"What are you talking about? I'm still in first gear."

As his heavier weight pulled him ahead, he glanced at Amy's face and laughed maniacally. Not to be outdone, Amy leaned down and forward to shift her weight downhill. With her diminutive size, the effort was of little use.

By the time they approached the bottom, Reed was well ahead. He leaned left to send the sled into a sideways slide intended to stop their progress. He slowed and Sammy hopped off. As Reed prepared to dismount, ready to do a victory dance with the little boy, Amy let out a warning squeal. Her sled plowed into him. Down he went. Amy's sled toppled over, spilling both occupants into the snow.

The next thing he knew, Reed was in a tangle of arms and legs and laughter with Amy.

"You big oaf," she said, swatting at his shoulder. Against his thick parka, the swats thudded painlessly. Snow glistened in her hair and melted on the warmth of her face.

"You were the lousy driver." Grinning, Reed reached up to dust the snow from her cheek. Their eyes met and held. Hers were blue and sparkling.

"You have snow..." She touched the corner of his mouth.

It was the perfect moment to kiss her again. From the look in her eyes, she wasn't averse to the idea. Maybe he'd moved too fast the first time. Today he'd leave the decision to her. Breath puffing, heart still pumping with adrenaline, he cupped her cheek. She looped a gloved hand around his neck and her lips curved. Beautiful lips, reddened from the wind and cold, and probably in need of warming.

"You gonna hit me?" he murmured, leaning closer.

Instead of words, Amy answered with action. She yanked his head down and kissed him—fast, sweet and briefly—then gave a great shove against his chest that sent him tumbling back into the snow.

He grabbed at her ankle as her feet spun, searching for purchase in the slick snow. Amidst the laughter and squeals, Dexter and Sammy catapulted into the fray.

An all-out snowball fight ensued. As Reed sat back on his heels, flinging snow and growling like a bear at the little boys, the need for family grew inside him. Not any family, but this one: Amy and Sammy and Dexter.

When they all collapsed, exhausted and breathless onto the ground, Sammy piled onto Reed's lap and hugged him. Reed looped an arm around Amy on one side and Dexter on the other. The rosy-cheeked child looked from one adult to the other and said, "Are you two getting married now?"

Reed's indrawn breath sucked in enough cold to make him cough. Thank goodness. Dexter's question had no answer. At least not yet.

He'd fouled things up pretty badly the day of Ben's death. He saw that now. Pushy, demanding, stunned with grief and guilt, he'd offered to marry Amy because of Ben. For a woman who loved the way Amy loved, his proposal had been nothing short of an insult. She'd never agree to a marriage of convenience, no matter how right it might be. No wonder she'd turned him down flat. But what about now that they'd spent time together, talked, shared, grown as people and, dare he think it, as a couple? Would Amy accept if he asked again? From her soft, bemused expression, Reed thought she might. Still, he, a normally decisive guy, wasn't certain.

So he took the easy way around Dexter's innocent question and didn't answer at all. Instead, he wrestled the child into the snow and let the moment pass.

The question didn't leave him, though.

If and when he proposed to Amy again, it would be for all the right reasons.

Chapter Twelve

The next Saturday dawned with skies white and heavy with forecast snow. Amy was determined that no amount of snow or cold weather would spoil the Christmas tree lighting.

"I can't wait to see the park all lit up for Christmas," she said to Lindy as they went over the last-minute details of tonight's event. Lindy owned a boardinghouse at the edge of town, and as such was active in Treasure Creek's government.

"We weren't planning to do any decorating until that treasure of yours was found." Lindy's short brown bob swung with the tilt of her head.

"I'm glad we didn't cancel, Lindy. Even if we're broke, we can still celebrate Christ's birth."

"But no one except you had the Christmas spirit." Behind brown frame glasses, Lindy's eyes were thoughtful. "We were all too down, I guess."

"Well, thank the sweet Lord Reed and Tucker found that long-hidden treasure chest. I'm still amazed by that. It couldn't have been anything but God answering a lot of prayers."

"You won't get any argument from me. I've never been much of a churchgoer, but I've sure seen a change in people. Since the treasure was found, we've all got a new attitude. Everyone is excited, smiling, helping each other out. Even

Cloris Beacher donated a few dollars to buy oranges for the goody sacks Santa's handing out tonight."

Amy grinned at the mention of the town's most renowned skinflint.

"See? Miracles do happen." She ripped a sheet of notes from her plan book, folded them and stuck them into the pocket of her puffy vest. "I think we're good to go, Lindy. You've done a fabulous job helping me put this together so quickly."

"Me? Honey, I don't know how you do all you do—the pageant next Sunday and the decorations today, the lighting tonight. Your business and the kids. And now you and the police chief are dating. I get tired just thinking about your schedule."

Amy didn't bother to deny the comment about her and Reed. She'd heard it repeatedly since they'd had dinner at Martelli's, and no one believed her denials anyway. Maybe even her.

Something had definitely changed between the two of them, at least for Amy. She was beginning to believe she could love again—maybe she already did—but she had to be sure Reed wanted her for herself and not because of the promise he'd made to Ben.

She glanced at the sunburst clock hanging above Lindy's desk. "The countdown begins. I'd better run home and get the boys bundled up. They are so excited about putting up the decorations in the park, seeing the live nativity and talking to Santa."

"See you in about an hour."

With that parting comment, Amy stepped out into falling snow and increased traffic flowing into Treasure Creek's main thoroughfare.

An hour later, Amy circulated among the decorators like a spinning top, stopping often to comment and admire. The town park bubbled with the season's cheer and the excitement and family feeling of the day's events.

This was the Treasure Creek Amy knew and loved—happy and safe. Even though Reed's investigation had turned up nothing about the break-in or the men who'd frightened her boys, trouble was the furthest thing from her mind.

Bethany and Nate untangled a huge box of lights positioned on the back of a pickup truck, while Casey and Jake began stringing them in loops next to evergreen boughs hung along the wrought-iron fence bordering the pretty little park.

Amy had shut the business offices for the day, so all her employees could participate in the decorations and tree lighting. Friends and community members swarmed the area, everyone pitching in where needed. Laughter and camaraderie punctuated their work.

City workers pounded a platform into place near a giant spruce that served each year as the town's official Christmas tree. From the platform, carolers and the high school band would perform, and Lindy had agreed to give the welcome before Santa, aka Harry Peterson, officially flipped the switch to light the tree.

From atop a cherry-picker truck, Andy Carlson looped lights on the massive spruce and parked a huge gold star on the top.

Ethan Eckles was setting up a sound system. After some feedback squeals that had everyone slapping hands over their ears, Christmas carols rang out from a boom box. Amy stopped on one of her rounds and thanked him.

He hadn't asked her out again since she and the boys had moved out to Reed's ranch, but Amy was determined not to have an issue with her friend and part-time employee. If Ethan's demeanor was a bit stiff at first, she understood.

"The choir will sing later during the lighting," he said. "But I thought some music while we work would be good."

"I'm glad you thought of it."

He clicked the CD onto "Joy to the World." The scar on his cheek puckered as his mouth curved. "Don't lie. It was on your list."

She laughed. It was. "But you saved me a phone call."

"That's what friends are for."

She walked away humming, feeling better about their friendship. The ladies' auxiliary group had set up a folding table and produced Christmas cookies and coffee to keep everyone going. After the lighting, they were all set to let children decorate cookies of their own. Amy sailed past and snitched a tempting snicker doodle. Jenny, the pastor's wife, swatted her hand playfully.

Heart as full as her mouth, Amy laughed with real pleasure at the way her little town had pulled together in the last year, especially now at Christmas. The best things in life really were free, a lesson she wanted to remember long after Treasure Creek had recovered from its recession.

Delilah Carrington came around the corner and nearly bumped into her. "Amy! Hello."

Amy was glad to see the other redhead looking more upbeat, though she couldn't help noticing how two men who'd been hanging lights on a storefront suddenly disappeared. She smiled. Delilah's reputation for being a man-hunter wouldn't die easily.

"How are things going? Have you heard from California yet?" Amy asked, hoping Delilah had heard from her friend Ronald.

Delilah's face fell.

"Nothing."

Amy's heart pinched. She touched Delilah's arm. "I'm sorry. I shouldn't have asked."

"Don't apologize. You asked because you care." The woman smiled a little too brightly. "But I'm okay. Really."

Amy wasn't convinced, but she smiled and waved as the woman headed on down the street toward the park. Delilah was hurting, but since coming to Treasure Creek she'd matured a lot. With God in her life and new friends at her side, she would be all right even if she wasn't married by Christmas as she'd hoped.

A short time later, Amy looked around for Reed and her sons. Sammy and Dexter had insisted on trailing the police chief when he wandered over to his office to check in with the deputy and make sure the town was secure and the event appropriately policed. He and a part-time deputy worked the streets while Deputy Ken Wallace manned the office in the unlikely event of a 9-1-1 call. Sammy and Dexter loved visiting the police station.

She spotted them coming toward her from across the street, Sammy on Reed's shoulders and Dexter holding on to Reed's hand. Cy trotted alongside Dexter, his noble nose touching the child's opposite hand. The scene put a hitch in her throat. She lifted a hand to wave. Did he have any idea how good he was for those boys?

When Sammy spotted her, his little legs kicked against Reed like a horseback rider.

"Mama!" he cried, as if he hadn't just seen her fifteen minutes ago. Using one strong hand, Reed swung her son to the ground. Sammy barreled toward her with Dexter hot on his heels.

"Mama. Mama. Chief Weed let me push his radio buttons."

"Me, too, Mama," Dexter said. "He let me talk. I said, 'Merry Christmas. This is the police station.'"

Amy smiled at Reed with gratitude. No doubt the caller had been a friend, but still, it was a sweet thing to do.

"Impressive." At that moment someone called her name.

She glanced to where Casey tied a big red bow onto a corner post.

Casey's brown hair bobbed as she waved. "We need one more of these bows and we'll be done. Who has them?"

"I'll check."

Reed's radio crackled. After a brief conversation, he said, "Fender bender down by the post office. Gotta go."

"You'll be back before the festivities begin, won't you?" She looked at her watch. "Less than thirty minutes left."

"I'll try." He leaned in and touched his lips to hers, then saluted and hurried off, Cy with him.

Amy stood for a moment in delighted shock, watching him walk away. Then, with the boys in tow, she moved through the gathering crowd. Even with the light snow falling, the park was filling with people quickly. Some arrived on foot, others by snowmobile, trucks and SUVs. Doors slammed, motors roared and exhaust mingled with the snowfall. Practically everyone in town would be here, and many from the outlying regions.

The last thought gave her a funny feeling. There had been no further threats, no sightings of the men who had frightened Sammy and Dexter, and with Reed constantly on guard she'd begun feeling safe. Still, a large crowd of people gave her pause.

Surely, though, with all these friends around, nothing could happen. The treasure was safe in Reed's office. The boys were safe with her. No one would cause a scene in public, especially this close to Christmas.

While she convinced herself, someone called her name again.

"Boys, stay close to Mama, okay?"

Two heads nodded and moved closer. "Okay."

Satisfied, Amy paused to talk with the band director,

who asked, "How many songs do you want before Santa arrives?"

She answered his question and moved on.

"Amy, the caroling choir is ready. How soon should we go on stage?"

She looked toward the platform. Andy gave her a thumbs-up. Everything was ready. "Go on up now and get in place. The band will start—" she checked her watch "—in five minutes."

She started to move around the carolers, weaving through a sea of gathering bodies. Children's excited voices filled the air. Some hopped up and down for warmth, others out of sheer excitement. Still others tossed snowballs and ran squealing across the open areas of the park. Amy smiled. All was well in Treasure Creek.

"Amy." Someone caught her by the arm and asked yet another question. She fielded it and several more as she made her way to the area alongside the big tree, where she gave last-minute instructions to three high school girls dressed as elves who would assist Harry in passing out bags of candy. Harry, renowned for being a curmudgeon much of the time, had donated most of the candy himself. And he never failed to surprise the entire town with his jolly portrayal of Santa. Amy had often wondered if Harry's real personality came out at Christmas.

A drumbeat signaled the start, and with a blast of trumpets the band struck up "Here Comes Santa Claus." The gathered crowd sang along as Lindy made her way onto the platform. Along a cleared path to the left of the giant spruce, Harry Peterson, dressed as Santa Claus, rode up on the town's fire truck. Amy couldn't help smiling at the woman next to him—Joleen Jones outfitted as rather attractive bleached-blonde Mrs. Santa.

"Look boys, here comes…" She glanced down to where

Sammy and Dexter had been not one minute ago. Only Sammy clung to her coat hem.

"Sammy, where's Dexter?" Her eyes searched the crowd, sure her oldest son was nearby. He had to be. "Did he run up to see Santa?"

Sammy's eyes widened at the anxiety in his mother's voice. He wagged his head back and forth. "Uh-uh."

"Where is he? Where did he go? The bathroom?" There were Porta-Potties lining one side of the park. The area was well lit, but it was not like Dexter to leave her side without permission. Still, he was a little boy, excited about Santa and tonight's events.

"No, Mama. That man took him."

Fingers of ice gripped Amy's spine.

"What man?" She grabbed her baby's coat-clad shoulders. "Sammy, what man are you talking about? Did Dexter leave with a man?"

Tears gathered in Sammy's eyes. "The man gave him candy and took him to Santa. I want to go, too, Mama. I want Santa."

Amy's knees trembled with the news. "Did you know the man? Who was it?"

Please God, let it be one of her guides or someone from the day care.

"I don't know. Can I have candy, too?"

Gripping Sammy's hand, Amy plowed through the crowd, searching for a small boy in a red cap. Concern quickly turned to panic. Where was he?

"Casey," she said, rushing toward her friend. "Have you seen Dexter?"

"Not in a few minutes. He's probably trying to get close to Santa." Casey smiled and pointed toward the red fire truck and bobbing white wig. "Look at that crush of kids."

"Sammy says a man took Dexter up there. I don't see him."

Casey spun around, eyes wide with concern. "A man. Who?"

"I don't know."

"Oh, Amy." Casey frowned, cheer turning to worry.

Jake Rodgers, standing next to her, reached for Casey's hand. "We'll start looking."

"I'm going to the bandstand." Mouth dry and fear rising inside like a sickness, she rushed forward. "Lindy."

The town councilwoman, standing to one side of the platform waiting for her big moment, heard Amy's cry and turned with a cheery smile.

Amy blurted, "I can't find my son."

"What?" Lindy leaned down, a hand to ear. "I can't hear you over this overachieving tuba player."

Amy leaped onto the bandstand and went straight for the microphone. The band director did a double take, then signaled an end to the song.

"Is something wrong?" he hissed.

Amy stepped up to the mike as the last notes faltered and died. She tried to keep the panic from her voice. There was no point causing a scene if Dexter was in the line of children. "Excuse the interruption, but has anyone seen Dexter? I can't find him. Dexter, if you're out there, come up here to Mama right now."

A murmur ran through the gathered throng. Heads turned, as if to look for the lost boy. Seconds passed. Seconds in which Amy prayed and hoped and waited. Heavy dread tightened Amy's stomach. He had to be here. Where else could he be?

After a frighteningly long minute, she leaped off the platform and grappled in her pocket for the cell phone.

Voices surrounded her, offering reassurance. "He's here somewhere, Amy."

"Probably out there throwing snowballs, and didn't hear you calling."

"He'll show up. Don't worry."

But she *was* worried. Everyone didn't know what she knew. That someone would do anything to get his or her hands on that treasure. Including harming a small boy.

The last thought shook her to the core. She jabbed at the numbers on the cell phone. Just then, the chief of police came into sight.

"Reed," she said, breathing a sigh of relief. "Thank You, Lord."

With a quick snap, she closed the small phone and hurried toward the one man she trusted most with her children. If anyone could help, Reed could. Fighting tears, she dragged the bewildered, whining Sammy along. From the expression on Reed's face, he'd heard her announcement. She tried to control her emotions, but when Reed was close enough to touch, she fell against him.

"I can't find Dexter," she said. "They were right beside me. I don't know what happened. You don't think someone—"

His strong hands gripped her arms and slowly set her away from him. Jaw like granite, he said the words that nearly broke her in two.

"Someone did."

Chapter Thirteen

With Amy trembling against him, Reed was so furious he thought his head might explode. How had this happened? How had he failed so miserably in his protection of Amy's son? If he got his hands on whoever did this…

More reluctantly than he'd ever done anything, he showed her a single piece of paper. "Frank Drew's boy handed this to me a minute ago. Some guy in a camo coat gave him five bucks to bring it to me or you."

Reed watched with churning gut as Amy's fingers trembled against the ransom note. "An even trade. The kid for the treasure. Expect my call." Her shattered gaze rose to his. "A ransom note. Oh, Reed, someone kidnapped my baby."

She buckled then, this strong, exuberant woman who could single-handedly turn a town from the brink of financial collapse. Reed yanked her against him, tempted to sweep her into his arms, draw his gun and go blasting through the crowd until someone returned their boy. He resisted the urge, knowing time was of the essence. Instead, he hoisted Sammy into his arms and guided the quaking Amy toward his SUV, nodding curtly to concerned friends who vowed to search for the missing boy.

"We'll find him, Amy," someone said. "He can't be far."

Reed didn't bother to stop with the truth—that Dexter was being held hostage.

Once he reached the car and loaded Amy and Sammy inside, he said, "Lock the doors and wait for that call. I'll make the announcement over the PA, get people organized to search, and be back. We'll start driving. If the call comes in, text me an SOS. Got it?"

"I need to look for him."

"You need to get yourself together first. Take a few minutes to calm down. Talk to Sammy. Get a good description. I'll be right back. Promise."

"Okay. Okay. You're right." Face stricken white with fear, she didn't argue.

"No matter what you do, you and Sammy sit tight. Do not unlock the door. Do not get out of this vehicle."

Amy nodded and pulled Sammy onto her lap, where she hooked one arm tightly around him. The sight tore at him. If he'd been with her… If he'd had his eyes on the kids the way he'd promised, this would not have happened.

"Find my baby, Reed."

Fury ripped through him like a freight train. He barely ground out the answer. "Count on it."

With increasing urgency, Reed jogged toward the now lighted Christmas tree and a merry, singing crowd that had no idea of the drama being played out in its midst. The irony was not lost on Reed. He tried to focus as a professional cop, but objectivity had escaped him. This was Dexter. And someone was going to pay.

Lord, help me find him, he prayed silently. Though he'd never done much for God, and didn't figure he'd earned the right to ask, he figured God would look out for a sweet little kid like Dexter.

Nearing the center of attraction, he spotted Santa. Harry Peterson had dismounted from the fire truck and was ho-ho-

ho-ing to a gang of gathered children. Reed's chest ached to know Sammy and Dexter were not among them. He took the microphone, and in his usual terse manner, announced the kidnapping.

"I need your help. We have a description of a man who threatened the James family and who may have done this." He pulled a folded paper from his pocket. Since the scare at the school yard, he'd kept a copy with him all the time. Just in case. He held it up. "If you think you may have seen him, say so. Better to be wrong than sorry. Otherwise, we need searchers to cover every inch of this town and to block the roads in and out."

The shocked crowd responded as he knew they would. This was no longer a case of a child lost in a friendly crowd. Someone had one of Amy's boys, and the citizens of Treasure Creek would not stand for such a crime. As soon as the ripple of shock subsided, they called a halt to the festivities.

Every man who'd ever worked for the Jameses stormed the bandstand to join search parties. Jake Rodgers shouted into the microphone, "Five thousand dollars to anyone who finds that child in the next fifteen minutes."

Satisfied that these rugged men and women would do their part, Reed left Jake in charge and headed back to his SUV to await the promised phone call.

He'd been gone less than ten minutes, but he knew before he ever reached the vehicle.

Amy and Sammy were gone.

"Where is it, lady? Tell me where to find the treasure and no one gets hurt." The sandy-haired man shoved a gun harder against her ribs.

She still couldn't believe this was happening. She'd been sitting in Reed's police SUV, praying for the call that never came, when the barrel of a gun appeared next to her window.

"Open the door or I'll shoot."

For a moment she'd frozen. Her inaction had infuriated the man.

"Open now or the kid gets it." He tilted the barrel toward Sammy.

She opened the door.

The cold metal gun pushed against her temple. Threatening to kill Sammy and Dexter if she so much as whispered, he'd ordered her out of the vehicle.

"Leave Sammy. Please," she begged. "Take me, but leave him here."

The man's face hardened. He grabbed Sammy and jabbed the gun against his neck. Sammy began to cry.

"Shut him up or he dies."

Scared out of her mind, Amy stroked Sammy's hair and whispered. "Shh. Quiet, baby. Please be quiet."

She tried to think, tried to remember what to do in such a terrible situation, but her brain could only see the cold barrel of a pistol pointed at her child. Every fiber of her motherly being wanted to grab the gun and fight for her baby, but she knew the effort could be disastrous.

This was her fault. All of it. If she'd been watching the boys the way she should have. If she hadn't been so busy with the festivities…

"Move it, lady. And be quiet about it. Anyone stops me, and the kid pays."

Numbly, she nodded. She had to think of some way out of this.

With Sammy in his arms, the gun secreted beneath her baby's coat, the man forced her away from the crowd and through the darkness to a filthy pickup truck. Amy knew better than to get into the vehicle, but what choice did she have? Sammy's life was at stake.

Her cell phone began to ring.

The kidnapper jerked, hard eyes narrowed in warning. "Don't answer that."

She glanced down at the caller ID. Reed. He must have returned to his SUV by now. Hope bloomed. Reed would find her. He wouldn't stop until he did. She prayed he was on time.

The ringing ceased. Sammy, stiff with fear, cut his eyes in her direction and whimpered.

"Don't cry, Sammy. Mama's here." That was the only comfort she could offer.

The sandy-haired man had seated Sammy on his lap behind the steering wheel, the gun firmly against his small, pale neck. A blast of heat from the vents stirred the stench of fast-food grease and her stomach roiled. Amy clasped a hand to her mouth, afraid she would throw up.

"Where's the money? The famous treasure?" The kidnapper jerked his head, the action jarring the weapon pointed at Sammy.

Amy had known fear in her life, but never anything like this. These were her children, heart of her heart, flesh of her flesh. If anything happened to one of them she could not go on. Blood roared against her temples and her stomach threatened revolt. She folded her hands in her lap to control the shaking—and to pray.

"Where's Dexter? Take me to my son first. Then I'll tell you where the treasure is."

The man snarled at her. "I make the rules, lady. You do as I say. Tell me where the treasure is or choose who dies first. The big one or the little one?"

Oh, God in Heaven. Help us.

"Please don't hurt my babies."

"All we want's the treasure. Tell us, and the kids live." He pulled the truck to the side of a deserted road, where he wrapped the gun arm around Sammy's waist and then fumbled in his jacket for a cell phone. "One call and you all go free. A sweet deal for everyone."

"You can have the treasure. I don't care. Just take me to my son." Dexter would be terrified by now. He was too smart not to understand what was happening.

The man's eyes flicked from the cell phone to her, and back again, as he texted something. Then, with a hard smirk, he sat back to wait.

The wait was torment.

In the dim glow of dashboard lights, the kidnapper looked cruel and desperate. She had no doubt he would do anything to get his hands on the treasure. If she told him the truth, that no one knew for certain what was inside the box, he wouldn't believe her. He, like the townspeople, thought the chest contained untold riches. She hoped they were right. Her family's lives now depended on it.

Though only seconds passed, they felt like years before he said, "My partner says he'll meet us."

"Where?"

His grin was evil. "Wherever you keep the treasure."

At this point, she'd have told him anything he asked. Money meant nothing without her babies. "It's at the police station."

"Police station?" The thug blinked, clearly not expecting this turn of events. "You call the cops off, you hear? Tell them to stay clear or all of you die."

"The police chief has the combination to the safe. No one else." She didn't know if that was true, but it was the only way she could think of to contact Reed. "You'll have to get it from him."

Amy shuddered, afraid she'd just put Reed in danger, too. But her only hope of help rested with the police chief.

The man cursed as he texted something else into his phone.

Then he started the truck, stirring the stench and heat once more as he drove through the falling snow back into town.

The cheerful twinkle of red and green Christmas lights was lost on Reed as he and Cy roared past storefronts toward his office. He glanced in his rearview mirror, relieved that no one followed. He had enough hostages to deal with as it was.

"We got trouble, Cy," he told the dog, ruminating out loud to keep his emotions under check. Amy's brief phone call had just about done him in. The kidnappers had her. He had about two more minutes to formulate a plan to save the three people he loved most on the planet.

There it was, and no time to deal with it. He loved Amy James and he loved Dexter and Sammy. This was no longer about duty. This was about love.

As he approached his office, he turned down the back alley and cut his lights, easing into his parking space as unobtrusively as possible. He had no idea what he'd find inside the station. He'd tried radioing his deputy, but there was no response. Not that unusual. Ken could be on a call out of range. But Reed had a bad feeling. He'd better be ready for anything.

As he eased out of the truck, he slid his service revolver from the shoulder holster. "Cy. Stay."

Cy whined, but stayed put. He wasn't a police dog. He was a friend. No use getting him shot.

With only the moon for illumination, Reed picked his way carefully across the piles of shoveled snow, hoping to see something through the back window. He saw only darkness.

Holding back a sigh, he slowly turned the doorknob, then waited. No sound came. He pushed the door open. When nothing and no one moved, he stepped inside the back room, an area he used for storage. If he moved quickly and quietly, he just might get the drop on them.

He took three silent steps through the darkness before a voice stopped him.

"I know you're there, Truscott. Put the gun on the floor before someone gets hurt."

The overhead light flipped on. Reed went cold all over. The sandy-haired man in Casey's drawing stood in front of him holding a gun. On Dexter.

"Dex. Where's your mom? Are you okay?" He moved toward the shivering boy, trying to keep his fury in check for Dexter's safety. The child's eyes were red-rimmed, his nose ran and tears stained his cheeks. Whatever he'd been through had terrified him. Reed wanted five minutes on even footing with this man. Five minutes to teach him not to threaten small children.

"Chief." Dexter's little voice quavered.

"Shut up, kid. And no funny stuff from you, Truscott," the man warned, as he backed out of the room with Dexter in front of him.

"Let the boy go. Take me instead."

"You're not near as valuable as the kid." The sandy-haired man motioned with the gun. A 9-mm Smith & Wesson. Reed owned one just like it. A deadly, deadly weapon. "Open the safe."

Reed stepped into the brightly lit office. Amy sat in a folding chair, her hands taped in front of her around Sammy. Behind them stood yet another man. Thirties, pockmarked, greedy eyes. Cigarette smoke circled around him. But it was the pistol pointed at Amy's skull that held Reed's attention.

"Chief Weed, I scared." Sammy sniffled, his little body jerking as though he'd been crying for a while. The sound pierced Reed's heart.

And in that tiny sound lay a truth he didn't want to face. He would never be the man Amy needed. He could never be a father to these boys. He was a failure. Pure and simple. When they'd needed him most, he'd let them down. All of them. Just like he'd done with Ben.

"You okay?" he asked Amy, his teeth gritting.

She nodded. "Just give them the treasure, Reed."

"Gladly. First, let the woman and kids leave," he said to pockmarks, gauging him to be the leader.

"Nope. Treasure first. Then they go free." Tone eerily chipper, the man offered an evil grin as he raised one hand and quirked a finger. "Pinky promise."

Reed controlled the urge to punch his leering face. Three lives depended on him. The wrong move now could cost more than he could afford to lose. "How do I know I can trust you?"

"You don't." Pockmarks waved the gun. "Quit stalling, before my finger gets itchy."

"Where's my deputy?"

The man's grin widened. "I think he may have met with a little problem. Seems to be tied up in one of your jail cells. Don't worry. He'll live—as long as we get what we want."

Thank You, God. Ken was alive. If he played the thieves' game, perhaps they'd all come out of here unharmed.

He scanned Amy's face one more time in silent question. He had to be sure she and the boys were all right. Amy's chin went up and her eyes flashed. Reed almost grinned. She was tough, his Amy.

No, not his. Never his.

Beaten in more ways than one, he moved toward the safe, taking care not to make any sudden moves. Sandy and pockmarks didn't need an excuse to hurt someone.

The safe was a tall, black, fireproof cabinet. A bomb couldn't open this safe. But love could.

He whirled the dial back and forth until the inner mechanism clicked. The sound was loud in the frightfully quiet office. He could feel the gunman behind him, could almost smell the anxious greed coming off him as thick as the stench of stale cigarettes. Most of all, he sensed fear and helplessness emanating from the people he loved most.

Hand on the safe handle, Reed glanced over his shoulder. "Turn the boy loose."

"Open the door and the kid is yours." He pushed Dexter forward, but held his upper arm in an iron grip.

Dexter began to sob.

Reed shoved the lever down with a loud *thwack* and the door swung open. Inside lay the treasure that promised to save a town, a treasure that men would kill for.

With a heavy heart, Reed removed the box and placed it on a table. "Come here, Dexter. Come to me now."

The man released Dexter and grabbed for the box. Dexter ran into Reed's open arms, his sturdy little body shaking. Reed heard Amy's tiny whimper of joy. Relief poured through him as he lifted Amy's child against his chest and held on for all he was worth. One down, two to go.

"Take it and leave," he said. "It's all yours."

Pockmarks jerked his chin toward the sandy-haired man. "Let's get out of here."

"What about them? We can't leave witnesses."

Reed stiffened. His blood ran cold.

"We got what we came for." Pockmarks moved toward the door, treasure chest under his arm. "They'll never find us where we're going. Come on, before the whole town shows up."

Sandy-hair grunted a note of disapproval, but followed. In seconds, they were gone, leaving only a blast of cold air.

Reed rushed to Amy's side and fell to his knees next to her chair, where he gently cut away the tape from her reddened wrists.

"Thank God," he choked in true gratitude, pulling her and both boys into an embrace that said everything he couldn't.

Amy quietly sobbed her relief against his shoulder. He stroked her back and her soft hair and wished he was half the man Ben had thought he was. His heart pounded, his gut churned and he was as near tears as he could ever remember. These three people were his heart and soul. He would do anything for them—and yet he hadn't.

Teeth gritted, he made a vow, and this time he would keep it no matter the cost to himself. Somehow, he would make this right.

And he'd start by bringing in the men who had threatened their lives and stolen their treasure.

Chapter Fourteen

"I'm going after them."

Reed's statement yanked Amy's head up. The relief she'd been feeling flew out the window. "You can't."

He carefully disentangled himself from the three Jameses. Amy clung, an action unlike her. She couldn't let him go. It was too dangerous.

"The treasure doesn't matter anymore."

Reed seemed oblivious to her plea. He stomped to the gun cabinet and extracted a rifle and shells. "I have to."

Fury came off him in waves and frightened Amy all over again. "We're safe now, Reed. That's the important thing. Let them go. They have guns. You could get hurt."

"I can't let them get away with this, Amy."

"You'll never find them in the dark."

"I'll find them." His jaw was like granite. "If I hurry. The snow is fresh."

"Please don't go."

"After what they did to you and the boys? What kind of police officer would I be if I let them walk away? What kind of *man* would I be?"

Amy had no answer. For a man with his pride and sense of duty, the response was clear. He had to try.

"Let Ken out." With a jerk of his chin, Reed indicated the keys on his desk. "I'll update him by radio when I can. Let Jake and the others know you and the boys are safe."

"Reed, wait." But he was already gone, storming out into the snowy night. She wanted him to hold her one more minute. She wanted to tell him how much he meant to her.

"Mommy." Sammy's voice was so small and worried, her heart ached. "Will the bad men hurt Chief Weed?"

"Chief Reed is a policeman, baby. He knows what to do."

"I'll pray," Dexter said. "I prayed when the bad man got me. I prayed for Chief Reed to come and he did."

"Oh, Dexter. Oh, my precious baby." She clung to her sons and wished she never had to let go. "Of course we must pray. Right now."

All three bowed their heads and murmured heartfelt prayers for Reed's safety. Afterward, Amy took the keys and went into the back portion of the station to release the deputy. He was tied and gagged and furious, but otherwise unharmed. One more thing to be thankful for. She gave him Reed's message and, as he left the police station, she punched in Casey's cell number. In minutes, Reed's office swarmed with the good citizens of Treasure Creek. One by one, her guides who'd been scouring the town arrived, too.

Casey hugged her hard, eyes red. "Thank God you and the kids are safe."

"They took the treasure," Amy said. "I'm sorry. I know everyone was counting on it."

"Honey, you had no choice." Lindy slapped a hand down on Reed's desk. "No amount of money is worth a hair on one of these boy's head."

Amy agreed, but she was glad to hear someone else say the words.

"She's right, Amy." Harry, still wearing a Santa suit, but

without his beard and wig, patted her hand. "I'll admit we had high hopes for that treasure of yours, but we'll survive without it. You just wait and see."

"We sure will." Joleen clung to Harry's arm. "Don't you worry your sweet little ol' self one more minute about that treasure. Why, the way this town has pulled together, we can do anything. Treasure or not."

Delilah slipped an arm over Amy's shoulders and hugged. "She's right, you know. We'll make it. You taught me that."

A murmur of agreement went around the room. Amy's emotions, already on overload, spilled into her eyes and down her cheeks. "You are the most incredible bunch of friends—"

Gage Parker cleared his throat. All eyes turned toward the search-and-rescue guide. "Folks, we got a man out there searching for a treasure and a couple of thieves. He needs help. Way I figure, there are several of us in this room who know the territory better than anyone, even Reed. What do you say, men?" He winked at Casey. "And lady?"

Amy gazed around at her gathered guides, Casey, Ethan, Andy and Nate. All of them nodded and moved forward to stand with Gage in a show of solidarity. "We're in."

"Me, too." Tucker Lawson stepped up. "I may not be a guide, but I've spent my share of time in the wilderness. I know the lay of the land."

This was true. He'd spent months alone in the Alaskan bush, after a near-deadly plane crash. Tucker knew his way around.

Pride swelled inside Amy until she thought she would burst. These were people a town could count on. And that was far more important than a burgeoning bank account.

Reed's windshield wipers beat a scratchy rhythm against the silent, falling snow. Thick and powdery, the snow collected in crusts on the warmed windshield. He reached to turn the defrosters up one notch, grateful for the strong blast of heat in this weather. With each mile that passed, each foot he climbed, the snowstorm worsened. Soon, the telling set of tracks he followed would disappear. Desperate to catch the thieves before that happened, he increased his speed. There was danger in the action, he knew, but with God's help he would not allow the men to get away.

Straining against the blinding snow and the deepening darkness, he peered far into the night, beyond the reach of the headlights. The road would run out soon, a hazard of living in Alaska. Roads were a luxury, not a given, as they were in the Lower 48. Tall trees rose on either side of what was now merely a narrowing trail. The dark, hulking mountains were before him, as was the treacherous Chilkoot Trail. Thousands of square miles of wooded, mountainous terrain spread around him in silent, sinister darkness.

The thieves no doubt would take the known trail for a while, but would quickly branch off into the wilderness to avoid capture. There were plenty of places to hide and make camp before crossing into Canada, where they could disappear forever. Reed wasn't about to let that happen.

He left the beaten track to guide the four-wheel drive down a rugged path through encroaching timber. The Explorer bounced, rattling the dashboard and radio equipment, as well as jarring his teeth. Cy offered several insulted sighs at the rough ride.

Several minutes later, he drove up on an abandoned pickup truck parked between two trees in plain sight. Either the thieves were foolhardy, or they were confident no one would follow this far into the wilderness—proof positive they didn't know Reed Truscott. Though his sense of urgency increased, Reed's four-wheel drive ground to a halt on the steep, snow-covered incline. Like the men he sought, he could drive no farther.

"Found 'em, Cy. Or at least their vehicle." He radioed to Ken. Though the connection was poor, he hoped the deputy understood his directions. His cell phone was as useless as his truck this far off the beaten track.

"This is it, buddy," he said to Cy. "Time to prove we're real Alaskans."

After bundling into his heaviest outerwear, he slid booties onto Cy's feet and followed the fading outline of two pairs of footprints. If he guessed right, the thieves had set up a hideout not far away. Only a pair of idiots would wander into the deep woods in this kind of weather without a planned stopping point. All the treasure on earth wouldn't do them any good if they froze to death.

Trudging through knee-deep snow, Reed shined a flashlight on the thick forest rising sharply ahead. He kept a close eye on Cy, who was his best protection against falling off a cliff or into a crevice. The dog, bred for Alaskan winters, darted ahead, tongue pumping, joyful to run and play in the cold.

Reed wished he could say the same. Snow stung his cheeks. His eyes watered from the sharp, cold wind, though the rest of him remained warm enough for now.

"Not as much fun as sledding with Amy," he mumbled.

Amy. Guilt seared him every time he thought of how badly he'd let her down. He promised she'd be safe with him. In his arrogance, he'd demanded she move into his house where he could protect her.

"Some bodyguard you are." He figured, if he'd ever had a chance with her, he'd blown it big-time today. "Sorry, Ben. I guess you picked the wrong friend."

The wind howled down from the mountains and circled through the trees, grabbing at him with icy fingers. He trudged on. He'd give himself another thirty minutes of tracking and then he'd return to the station. Getting lost out here was easy to do. He'd never catch anyone if that happened.

Snow crusted his eyelashes. Not good. He wiped it away with his thick, waterproof glove. His hands were starting to chill now. So were his feet.

He thought of Amy's wacky heated socks and smiled. Not a bad idea tonight.

After a while, he paused next to a tree to shine his light in a broad sweep. His time was running out. He couldn't go much farther.

A movement to the right whirled him in that direction. Cy, too, spotted the movement and growled. Breath held, Reed snapped off his light.

"Easy boy," he whispered. "Don't give us away."

He hoped the flashlight hadn't already done as much. Heart thudding against his ribs, Reed moved silently from tree to tree. Fifty yards ahead, a dark, bulky shape indicated a hut of some sort. A tiny light, perhaps a candle, flickered inside.

"Bingo," he mouthed.

He approached the hut with caution, aware that both men had weapons and were just crazy enough to use them. A dead police officer dragged far enough into the woods might not be found until spring, if ever. And Reed wasn't planning on dying tonight. He had a bone to pick with these two.

The hut appeared old and unused, and it was not much more than a leaning set of four walls and a roof, maybe a relic from the Gold Rush days. Such warming huts dotted the Alaskan wilderness, especially along the Chilkoot and Klondike trails. This one was a little too far off the track to be used much, which explained its poor condition.

There was only one entrance, and no windows in the tiny shack. He'd have no choice but to walk right in the front door or wait for them to come out. Waiting in this weather was out of the question.

He pressed his radio. Nothing. No backup.

He signaled Cy to stay by the tree. Satisfied the malamute

would obey, Reed drew his weapon and approached the hut. A drumbeat of tension pounded in his temples. He'd only have one chance at a surprise attack.

He counted to three and shoved the door open. The bang ricocheted like a shotgun blast.

What happened next would always be a blur in his memory. The two men were on their knees in front of a small fireplace, frantically blowing on the hint of a fire. At Reed's entrance, both jerked to their feet and spun, faces stunned. Pockmarks grappled at his side, presumably for his weapon. Sandy dashed into the shadows.

Cold and tired and still mad enough to eat nails, Reed was in no mood. "Move again and I'll shoot."

Pockmarks yanked his arms above his head.

Somewhere to his right, Reed felt the presence of the sandy-haired accomplice, but in the semidarkness, he couldn't see him. That made him nervous.

"You," he said, indicating the place he assumed Sandy to be. "Move over here, hands up where I can see them."

He reached in his pocket for a set of handcuffs. As he moved to secure the pockmarked thief, he heard a pop. Then the world went crazy.

The bullet's impact spun him sideways. The handcuffs flew from his fingers. Unbalanced, he went down. As he fell, he kicked his legs, catching pockmarks off guard. The man plummeted face-first, where he struck his head against the rock fireplace and lay still.

A gun popped again.

Reed rolled, sure he was hit but feeling nothing but wild fury and powerful determination. If he made it out of this alive, he'd beg Amy's forgiveness and tell her everything that was in his heart. If she walked out, so be it. At least she'd know he loved her.

Another shot rang out. Rolling, determined not to be an

easy mark, Reed desperately tried to locate his attacker in the nearly dark room. He blinked away the fuzziness, fighting the fog that had moved into his head.

Suddenly, a deep growl pierced the night. In a flurry of fur, Cy sprang from the doorway like a crouched cougar. A man screamed, high and frightened above the dog's growl. Reed could hear the struggle of man and canine as Cy's powerful teeth found their mark. Still, the dog was in danger. No matter how great Cy's courage, the human had a gun. Cy didn't.

Reed struggled to his feet. His head swam crazily. He blinked away the gray spots as he reached into his boot for a second, smaller pistol. With effort, he stumbled toward the dark figures struggling on the cabin floor. If he wasn't so tired, he would have grinned. Cy was winning.

At Reed's appearance, Cy's fury increased. The man screamed and flung one arm over his eyes. "Get him off. Get him off!"

"Cy, come." Reed shoved one boot onto the man's chest and pointed the revolver at his face. "You stay."

"Keep the dog off me. I'm bleeding. He bit me."

"Hands behind your back. *Now.*" While he handcuffed the criminal, Cy sat nearby, growling menacingly. "Watch him, Cy."

He needn't have spoken, because the dog wasn't taking his one good eye off the man. Every hair on the malamute's thick coat stood at attention. If Sandy moved, he'd pay the price.

Strangely weak, but running on adrenaline, Reed wobbled to where the other man had begun to stir. Still facedown, the thief moaned softly. Reed yanked his limp hands behind his back and secured him, too. By the time he'd finished, he was badly winded.

He tried to shake away the double vision, but the effort was too much. He sagged over the criminal, panting.

Given the strange, stinging sensation in his thigh, he knew

he'd taken a bullet there. Maybe another in his side. How badly, he couldn't guess, and he was too weak to look. Somehow, he'd get these two back to the SUV and radio for help.

He started toward the open door, wobbled, shook it off, took one more step, then went to his knees. He put both hands against the cold floor, short of air. Weak. So weak. Maybe he should rest. Just for a minute.

Wind and snow blew into the hut, chilling him. Someone moaned. Him? Cy moved against him, licked his face with a warm, wet whine. Reed tried again to get up and failed. This time he crawled to the door, managed to push it shut, though he felt as weak as a baby kitten. Chest heaving, he leaned his back against the wall and trained his weapon on the bad guys.

Amy would have her treasure after all. Amy would be happy. He imagined her smile and smiled back. He heard her laugh and closed his eyes to absorb the beautiful sound. Amy floated in front of him. Ben was there, too, smiling.

Ben? Smiling at *him?* Wasn't he angry for the way Reed had failed?

Cy licked his face again and whined. No use, buddy, Reed wanted to say, but his mouth was too dry. He shivered. Cold. So cold.

A voice jerked him awake. Had he dozed? The gun remained in his hand, pointed at the crooks. He was okay. He was alert. Doing his duty.

"Do it right or get out of the way," he heard his father say. "Worthless weakling."

No, not his father. Couldn't be.

Who was talking? He wasn't sure. The crooks? Must be. Plotting. They'd make their move if he passed out. He'd be dead and forgotten. Amy would never know. She'd never get her treasure back.

She smiled again, assuring him that all was well. He leaned into the feeling, content.

And that was the last thing he remembered.

Chapter Fifteen

"Amy, you'd better come with us."

Amy raised her head from a hard, wooden surface and looked up into the exhausted face of Gage Parker.

She had fallen asleep praying, her forehead on Reed's desk. Sammy and Dexter were crashed out on the floor, snuggled in a stack of jailhouse blankets.

Several friends, including the pastor and his wife, sat in chairs around the office, reading or talking quietly. A fresh pot of coffee fragranced the air. Bethany was pouring herself a cup.

Bless them. No one wanted to leave until Reed returned safe and sound.

"Is Reed back? Did you find him?"

Casey, Nate and Jake, along with Deputy Ken Wallace, circled her chair like a wall. No one was smiling in triumph.

"We found him." Gage's terse reply was no comfort. Something was wrong.

Alarm zinged through her, stinging her nerve endings. She cast a quick look at her boys, wanting to shield them from any further bad news. Even after all the trauma they'd been through tonight, they were still able to sleep in innocent peace. Thank goodness.

"Where is he?" She pushed up from the chair.

Casey grabbed her hand and squeezed. "He's at Doc Logan's place."

Amy's hand went to her throat. "Doc Logan's? Is he hurt? What happened?"

"They shot him."

Fear raced up her spine and circled inside her brain like a vulture, black and dangerous. "No. No."

"He lost a lot of blood before we found him." Gage's face was grim. Too grim.

"What does Doc say? He'll be okay, won't he? Where was he shot? How could this happen?" Reed was strong as a moose. Nothing could hurt him. Before anyone could answer her blast of questions, she started moving. "Take me over there, Nate. My car is still at the park. Will you take care of my boys?" She directed this last to Casey.

"You know I will. They'll be at my house. Go on now. He was still unconscious when we left. Doc couldn't tell us much, but Reed needs you."

Big, tough, confident Reed Truscott needed her. And oh, how she needed him. He couldn't die. Not now. Not when she'd fallen so completely in love with him. Not when she needed him so badly.

"Call Reed's granny."

Casey nodded. "Will do."

As fast as her high energy could move, Amy rammed her arms into a coat and swirled a colorful scarf around her neck.

"Let's go." She yanked the door open, oblivious to the blast of cold air, and ran for Nate's truck.

Though it was long after closing time, lights beamed onto the quiet, otherwise dark street outside Doc Logan's clinic. With no hospital in town, the older physician could be depended upon to attend after-hours complaints.

On the way over, Amy learned the story. Reed had been shot but managed to apprehend the criminals and regain the treasure chest. The fact that someone had found him at all, as far into the bush as he'd gone, was nothing short of a Christmas miracle.

Nate kept assuring her that Reed was tough. He would be all right, but she had to see for herself. She had to look into that beloved face and know he would live.

Not waiting for Nate's truck to stop rocking, Amy bolted out of the passenger's seat. Her boots slid on the icy parking spot. She caught herself on the truck door and tried again.

"Careful. You don't need a broken ankle." Nate's gravelly bark told of his concern. He got out more slowly, probably exhausted from the search. Bethany had come with them, and slid out behind Amy. She'd been unusually quiet all the way over to the clinic, and Amy knew she must be praying.

The threesome entered the clinic together and found it empty except for Reed's dog. Cy was sitting at attention, focus trained on something down the hall—probably his wounded master. The knowledge sent a shaft of compassion through Amy. Cy adored Reed. He'd be lost without the tall lawman. So would she.

When the malamute saw Amy, he leaped up and yipped once. She reached to pet his head, then gasped and yanked her hand away.

"He's hurt."

Nate touched her arm. "No."

"But he's bleeding. Look." She pointed at the thick fur matted with dark red. "All over his face and side."

A beat passed before Nate answered. "Doc checked him over. It's not his blood."

Amy's fingers flew to her lips. She made a small sound of

distress. The blood was Reed's. *Reed's.* The knot of tension in her stomach rose to clog her throat.

"There's so much. He lost so much."

Nate's gaze slid to a pale Bethany, and then back to Amy. "When we found him, Reed was propped against a wall holding a gun on two hog-tied prisoners. The fools didn't know he was unconscious. Cy had positioned himself over and around Reed. For warmth, I guess, but Doc says the pressure slowed the bleeding. Reed would have either died of exposure or bled to death before we found him, if not for the dog."

"Oh, Cy." She stroked the noble muzzle with both hands. Cy whined softly. Amy understood the feeling. The man they both loved was in jeopardy.

"Cy growled us off when we first arrived," Nate was saying. "He wouldn't let us near Reed until Casey came in and spoke to him."

"But he's such a gentle dog."

"Not when it comes to protecting his own."

The comment caught her right in the center of her heart, like an arrow to a bull's-eye. Cy was like his owner. He would protect his own, regardless of the cost.

"I have to see him. Where is he? Where is Doc?"

"I'm right here, missus." Doc Logan, wearing a flannel plaid shirt and looking nothing like a doctor, trudged down the hall. He was drying his hands on a green towel.

"How is Reed?"

"Took two bullets. One through the thigh and another grazed his side. Nicked a bleeder. Good thing I keep frozen blood on hand, or he'd be in trouble. His good physical condition is in his favor. He has a mighty good pal in that dog of his, too."

"Nate told me."

Doc nodded. "He'll have to take it easy for a while, build up his strength, but barring any unexpected infection, he should recover. Lucky man, I'd say."

Relief flowed over Amy like a warm summer breeze. She breathed a silent prayer of thanks, certain that luck had nothing to do with Reed's condition. God had been out there in that wilderness. God had heard their prayers. In the thousands of square miles of trees, mountains and wild, frozen terrain, the guides of Treasure Creek had been guided by a power greater than their own considerable knowledge.

"May I see him?"

"Won't do much good. I dosed him up with pain medication. Weak as he is, he might be out all night."

"I don't care. I need to see him."

"Figured you'd say that. You always were a fiery one." This trusted doctor who'd delivered both her sons pushed a booted toe against the lever of a plastic-draped bin and tossed in the green towel. The lid banged shut. "Go on back. He's in the infirmary."

Amy dispensed with niceties and flung herself down the hallway. Against the tile floor, her boots echoed the frantic pounding of her heart.

In a town as small as Treasure Creek, the small doctor's office, with a couple of beds separated by a curtain, was the best they could do. Anything too serious for Doc Logan was flown to a larger town. The thought eased some of her anxiety. If Reed was critical, Doc would have called a plane to fly him out.

The door to the room stood open, with Reed in plain sight. One look at the police chief lying still against the white sheets scared her all over again. Thick, dark blood dripped from a plastic bag and flowed through a tube into his left arm. A waxy pallor seeped beneath his naturally tanned skin. His dark, spiky lashes rested against his cheekbones, still as death itself. Pain tightened the corners of his mouth, a mouth she'd kissed ever so briefly. For a big, powerful man, Reed looked as vulnerable as a little boy.

"Reed," she said softly, approaching the bed. He was wearing a hospital-type gown. A layer of clean white blankets covered him to midchest. She didn't want to notice the bloodied clothes and blankets stuffed into a plastic bag next to the bed.

"Reed."

He didn't stir.

She leaned over him, touched his face, smoothed his hair back from his forehead, letting her hand linger there against the warm scalp. "Reed."

Still no movement.

"You big, foolish oaf," she choked. "I told you not to go. Now look at you. You could have died and no one would have ever found you. And for what? Money? I don't care about that dumb treasure. The town doesn't care, either. They care about *you*. You're not invincible, you know. Even super cops get killed." The last word caught on a sob she'd resisted for hours.

"Please wake up, Reed. I have so much to tell you. All this time I've thought you wanted to marry me because of your silly promise to Ben. Maybe you do, but I don't care anymore. I need you so much. Sammy and Dexter need you, too. They love you, you know." She sniffed, swiped at her eyes with a sleeve. "Me, too. I love you."

Not knowing what else to do, Amy leaned her head against Reed's chest and took comfort in the beat of his heart. The steady symbol of life was lovelier than a Christmas carol.

Reed's head hurt and his leg throbbed like a teenager's boom box. He was tempted to return to the oblivion behind his eyes, but a familiar voice intruded. He loved that voice.

Straining to hear, he swam up through the thick fog to

listen. *Amy.* He sighed. Amy was here again. She'd stayed with him in the cabin, and her smile had given him a reason to keep fighting against the blackness.

A dream, he supposed, but such a good one. The voice came again, declaring her love for him.

Yep, no doubt about it. He was dreaming.

"Wake up, Reed. Please wake up. Don't leave me."

Amy needed him.

"Coming," he tried to say, uncertain if the word was spoken or only thought.

Her cool, soft hand touched his face, stroked his hair. He felt a tear against his neck. Amy was crying. That wouldn't do. No one made Amy cry on *his* watch.

He fought the darkness, and slowly, slowly surfaced. He could hear Amy talking a mile a minute and then she stopped.

Sensation returned to his floating body. Pain, warmth. Oh, blessed warmth. And Amy's head resting on his chest.

He lifted a hand and stroked her hair. "You have beautiful hair."

"Reed!" She sprang upward. "You're awake."

She inched away, and he felt the loss clear to his tingling toes. His eyes fluttered open. He closed them again against the blinding white light, and then tried again. She was there at his side, looking down at him with red-rimmed eyes filled with love.

"You love me." His tongue was thick and seemed to have a mind of its own.

Amy's stubborn little chin—how he loved that chin—poked out. "I do. And I think you love me, too."

His mouth curved. This was his Amy. Take the moose by the antlers and make him cry uncle.

Though the action required more strength than he knew

he had, Reed hooked an arm around her neck and yanked her face to his. "You're right. I do."

And then he kissed her—really kissed her—the way he'd wanted to for nearly a year.

Amy's heart sailed upward like a hot-air balloon. How could she have been blind for so long? Reed Truscott loved her. Not for any reason other than herself.

When the kiss ended—too soon for Amy—she was reluctant to move away. Being held in Reed's arms, knowing he was alive and safe, and that he loved her for the right reasons, filled all the empty places inside.

She tilted back ever so slightly, to look at his beloved face.

"Say it again," Reed demanded.

Amy's mouth curved. She knew what he meant, but she teased, "Say what?"

His soft, dark eyes narrowed. He tugged at her hair. "You know."

"Oh, you mean that little part about love?"

"Yeah." His lashes fluttered down and he sighed. "You don't know how long I've waited, how long I've hoped to hear those words."

At his admission, wonder and joy splashed in the center of Amy's heart. "Why didn't you tell me? Why did you say it was because of Ben?"

He gave a short, breathy snort. "Because I was scared. Scared you would think I'd moved too fast. Scared you wouldn't feel the same. The first proposal was for Ben, and maybe out of grief and stupidity, but not the second. Or the third. You..." He chuffed again. "I could no more keep from falling in love with you than Cy can play trombone."

Amy laughed softly, thrilled to know how wrong she'd been. Reed loved her for herself, not out of duty.

"I thought I couldn't love anyone after Ben died, but I do." She stroked the whisker-rough outline of his jaw and reveled in the way he hung on her every word. This strong, self-sufficient man needed her. "I love you. Not because Ben wanted me to. Not because of the boys. Not for any reason except you. You're my hero. You have been for a long time, but tonight I finally broke past the confusion and understood the truth."

"What truth?"

"That it's okay for me to love again. Not only okay, but right and good."

His chest rose and fell. "You're not angry?"

"Not even close. Why would I be angry?"

"Lots of reasons." His jaw tightened beneath her fingertips. "One, I promised to protect you."

"And you did. When I was in that truck with the kidnapper, all I could think of was contacting you. I knew you'd come. I knew you'd find us."

Reed took a deep breath and slowly released it. "I died a thousand deaths knowing you and the boys were in danger. If anything had happened..."

"But it didn't. We're safe. You're safe. Though I might be a little mad at you for going after those goons." She gave a mock pout, then laughed. "Don't ever scare me like that again."

He pulled her hand against his heart. "Feel that? It beats for you. Ben was my best friend. I would have done anything for him. But you're my heart. You and Sammy and Dexter."

Amy melted. "The boys love you, too. Ben was right. They need you."

"What about you, Amy? Do you need me? I'm no prize, but if you'll have me, I'll spend the rest of my life loving you." His fingers tightened on hers. "Marry me. Not because of Ben. But because I love you with everything I have in me."

Amy's pulse stopped, then started again with an erratic

rattle. Reed, who rarely strung ten words together, had just made the sweetest speech she'd ever heard. In answer, she leaned in close.

Her "yes" was swallowed up in a kiss.

Chapter Sixteen

Nerves and excitement quivered through the Treasure Creek Christian Church fellowship hall like an earthquake tremor. Christmas Eve had finally arrived. After weeks of practice and hours of preparing sets and costumes, the Christmas extravaganza was about to commence. Afterward, the whole town would gather for potluck and the opening of Mack Tanner's treasure.

After the close call with her sons and Reed, Amy had a great deal to celebrate.

At the moment, fifty jittery cast members roamed the fellowship hall in costumes of biblical times, making last-minute preparations. Everything was set, except for one missing person—the narrator.

"Anyone heard from Kurt?" she said, raising her voice to be heard above the din.

"Not yet. He'll be here. Don't worry."

But she was. She could do the narration herself, but Kurt's rich voice was such a nice addition. If he wasn't here soon, she'd give him a call.

"Twenty minutes to showtime."

Ethan Eckles's announcement was met with increased twittering and a nervous *eek* from Joleen Jones. Harry Peterson, who never seemed to be far away from the fluffy blonde, patted her shoulder and whispered something in her ear. Joleen giggled and squeezed his arm. The store owner beamed as though he'd struck gold in the Klondike. Maybe he had.

Amy smiled at the unlikely, but clearly besotted pair. Love was in bloom all over Treasure Creek. She went down the hall to peek in at the sanctuary where Reed, Granny and her two sons were already seated, awaiting the program. Dressed in their Christmas best, Sammy and Dexter sat on either side of Reed, each striving for his attention. Reed, still recovering from his gunshot, but getting stronger every day, looked up and caught her watching. She waggled her fingers at him. He gave her a smile, then bent toward his grandmother and said something. Seconds later, he pushed out of the pew and came toward her.

"Is something wrong?" she asked.

"Can't a man in love talk to his best girl without something being wrong?"

Careful of his bandage, Amy threw her arms around his waist and hugged. He smelled good, like all of the Alaskan outdoors, with a touch of manly cologne.

Reed drew her near and kissed the top of her hair. "You look beautiful tonight."

"Hey, what's going on out here?" This from Dr. Alex Havens. Dressed as one of the magi, the pediatrician grinned through his fake beard. "Any hugging going on, I'll have to find my wife."

Alex had married his nurse, one of the newcomers to Treasure Creek.

"Where is Maryanne, anyway?" Amy asked.

"Right here." The petite brunette edged up behind her husband and circled his waist with her arms. "I've always wanted to hug a wise man." To Amy she said, "Isn't love grand?"

"Oh, yeah." Amy smiled. Anyone with eyes could see how much she loved her lawman.

"We hear congratulations are in order," Alex said.

The pediatrician wasn't the first that night to say the words, and Amy knew he wouldn't be the last. Word had spread quickly, as it tended to do in Treasure Creek. Amy and Reed were engaged.

"You heard right." Reed slid an arm around Amy and gazed down at her with a look that could melt a glacier. "I had to get shot to win her over, but she's worth it."

The other couple chuckled. Reed didn't know it yet, but the town council had nominated him for a special citation from the governor.

Amy wasn't amused, but she knew Reed. Embarrassed at the attention, he played down his heroics. But he was a hero, not only to her, but to everyone in Treasure Creek. He might as well get used to it.

"When's the wedding?" Maryanne asked.

"As soon as Reed is fully recovered," Amy said.

"Can't be soon enough for me," Reed said. And the admission was like warm chocolate to Amy's soul.

"You'll have to invite the whole town, you know," Maryanne said.

Amy had been thinking about that, and wasn't sure what to do. "In which case, it would have to be held in the middle of Main Street!"

"Hey, that could work. How about tomorrow?" Reed laughed at the look both women gave him.

Talking about weddings and the treasure that had caused so much trouble and excitement, the foursome fell into step and returned to the fellowship hall. As much as she wanted to think about married life with Reed, right now she had a pageant to put on.

"About time, isn't it, Amy?" Karenna Parker asked.

She glanced at her watch. "Ten minutes and counting." Oh, where was her narrator?

She stepped to the front of the long room and clapped her hands. After a minute and a round of *shhhs,* the room quieted.

"Tonight we honor our Savior's birth. All of you have worked so hard to make this pageant special for Treasure Creek, but especially for our Lord. Thank you. And remember, after the program we're all meeting back in here for a very special Christmas gift."

"The treasure," someone muttered. Several others asked after Reed's health and expressed their continued shock about the kidnapping.

"Yes, the treasure. After what it nearly cost us, we have a lot to be thankful for," Amy said. "So, if everyone is ready—"

Before she could finish her sentence, the side door banged open, rattling the wall. A tall, thin man with brown plastic glasses, a shock of brown hair flopping around his ears and a determined look stormed into the fellowship hall. Reed bristled and stepped in front of Amy, one hand inside his jacket. The thieves were miles away, in county jail awaiting trial, but with the treasure being opened tonight, Reed was taking no chances.

"Where is she?" the man cried, loud enough to stun fifty people into silence. "Where is Delilah? Where is my woman?"

"Ronnie?" A voice shrieked from the anteroom, where the players had been getting dressed. A scurry of movement, and then the crowd parted as Delilah Carrington, dressed as an angel, fluttered toward the thin man. "Is it really you?"

The man stopped as though stunned by her appearance. She was spectacular. Small and elegant, with red ringlets and flawless complexion beneath a halo, and wearing a flowing, gossamer gown that only Delilah could make work, she was lovely looking.

"My angel," he said in a voice of awe and love. "My beautiful Delilah."

"Ronald Pfifer," Amy whispered. It had to be. Big nose, thick glasses and skinny arms, here was the computer nerd that Delilah had left behind and now pined for.

Delilah extended a hand and touched him. Her glittery, feathered wings fluttered. "You've come. Oh, Ronald. I made a terrible mistake. Please forgive me."

The man's Adam's apple bobbed as he clasped the extended, perfectly manicured fingers. "There's no Delete for me and you, Delilah. You're on my hard drive forever, password protected. You're my everything. Always have been. I love you, woman." He dropped to one knee and fumbled in his jacket pocket. "Marry me, my angel."

Ronald Pfifer, windblown and red-eyed after what must have been a long, arduous journey from California, had thrown caution out the door to declare his love in front of a roomful of strangers.

While those strangers held their collective breath, the fancy woman who'd come man-hunting to Treasure Creek slipped to her knees in front of the man she'd loved all along. Her gown rustled, her wings glittered beneath the light, but it was the look on her face, humbled and loving, that held Amy spellbound.

"I never should have left. You were always the one, Ronnie. I was blind and silly to go searching for the end of the rainbow, when the pot of gold was in my own backyard. I'm lost without you."

Ronald's smile was tender and filled with joy. "Me, too." And he slid a stunning diamond onto her trembling, outstretched hand. "Come here, baby. Let Ronnie take care of you."

Delilah fell into his arms, laughing and crying. The onlookers broke into cheering applause. Though they didn't know him from Adam, the men pounded Ronald's thin back and the women circled Delilah for hugs and to gush over her ring.

When the twitter of excitement subsided, Harry Peterson cleared his throat.

"Congratulations to this young man and Miss Delilah. Nothing like love to make Christmas sweeter than ever. Which brings me to my announcement." Harry smiled down at another, smaller and fluffier angel, Joleen Jones. They stood with arms around each other's waists, smiling secretively. "This pretty lady has agreed to be my wife. I figure that's a Christmas miracle right there." His grin widened. "And I'm offering a ten percent discount on everything at the store all month long to celebrate."

"Isn't he romantic?" Joleen gushed.

Along with everyone else, Amy laughed. The whole town had known it was just a matter of time before the store owner popped the question. That he'd announced his intentions here, in front of everyone, showed just how hard he'd fallen for the Southern belle.

The door opened again and Pastor Ed stuck his head inside. "The church is packed. Are you ready to begin?"

Someone told him about the newly engaged couples, and he stepped inside for the proper niceties. Amy, meanwhile, searched the hallway for a sign of her missing narrator.

"What's wrong?" Reed's voice rumbled behind her.

"Kurt isn't here yet. And he's the narrator. We can't start without him." She took out her cell phone and made the call. When the brief conversation ended, Amy's shoulders sagged. "He has laryngitis. His wife said he'd been trying every remedy, convinced he'd recover in time for the pageant, but nothing has worked."

She rubbed the spot between her eyebrows. Everything had been going so well.

"I'll do it."

Hope hippity-hopped like a bunny. Reed's warm, smooth baritone would be perfect, and the job wouldn't overtax him, though Amy was not about to say that to Reed. He was a little embarrassed about his weakness as it was. She thought he should have taken a month's vacation and stayed in bed. He was back at work three days after being shot.

"Seriously? You'd do this?"

He shrugged. "I can't promise perfection, but I can read."

She'd listened often and with love to his rich voice reading bedtime stories to her boys. He would do a beautiful job.

"I know public speaking isn't your thing."

"No, but you are." He smiled and Amy's heart responded. How she loved this man. He stepped closer, so that they were a heartbeat apart. "Don't you get it, Amy? I'd do anything for you."

In front of the waiting cast, Amy tiptoed up to plant a kiss on his cheek and whisper. "I love you."

Reed's eyes twinkled. "That's all I needed to hear. Give me that script." He winked. "And look out, Hollywood."

The pageant came off without another hitch.

Beneath dimmed lights, the ancient story of Jesus's birth played out with a beauty and sweetness that stung Amy's eyes.

She wasn't the only one. As the chief of police narrated the events, and the choir rose in collective voice to herald the birth of the King, no one noticed the flat notes or the slightly worn choir robes. The modern world faded away, and the old church in Treasure Creek was transported to a stable in Bethlehem.

As Mary knelt beside her newborn son and Joseph looked on in reverence, Karenna's sweet soprano sang "Mary, Did You Know."

Though Amy had heard the song dozens of times, chills ran down her arms at the line, "when you kissed your little baby, you kissed the face of God."

At the end of Karenna's song the cast remained in place, frozen in time and holiness, as the lights went out in the sanctuary. The only light was that of the star, shining brightly over the stable and the holy child.

A hushed reverence fell over the worshippers as each adult lit a candle, then passed the flame to the next person.

In moments, the church glowed with candlelight. Pastor Ed stepped to the microphone and quietly read, "'For unto us a child is born, unto us a son is given; and the government shall be upon his shoulder; and his name shall be called Wonderful, Counselor, The Mighty God, The Everlasting Father, The Prince of Peace.'"

He closed the Bible and took up his lighted candle. "As we conclude this beautiful service, may the Prince of Peace be with all of you tonight and in this coming New Year. And though we will extinguish our candles, may the light of His love continue to shine in your hearts and live forevermore."

He blew out his candle. All around the room the flames flickered and died. The houselights came up, but the people remained quiet and respectful, almost as if they had truly witnessed the birth of the Christ.

Amy stood in the wings and wept for joy.

Long after the stage cleared and the town gathered in the fellowship hall for refreshments and the opening of the treasure, the mood remained subdued but joyous.

"Beautiful program, Amy." Penelope Lear, gorgeous in red, sparkling Christmas attire, repeated a phrase Amy had heard over and over. Beside her, Tucker Lawson nodded his agreement.

"It was, wasn't it?" And she took no credit for it. God's spirit had been in the program. Plain and simple.

She squeezed Reed's hand. His narration had been perfect and she'd told him so.

"Want something to drink before the big moment?" he asked. He'd left a few minutes ago and returned with Mack Tanner's treasure. Now the chest sat in the center of the room on a table.

"No. Too excited. I just know God is about to gift this town with something truly amazing."

"I think He already has."

She smiled. Yes, Reed was right. Regardless of what was in the treasure chest, the little town of Treasure Creek was blessed.

"Let's do it, shall we?" Still holding his hand, she moved to the table. The gathered townspeople made way and began to circle the table in anticipation. The room was packed with people flowing out into the hallways, the balcony and the sanctuary.

Her guides and friends stood the closest, with Nate and Bethany to her right, Casey and Jake to her left, and her little boys clinging to her crushed velvet dress. She didn't know if she would ever be able to let them out of her sight again.

"Okay, everyone, the time has come to open my great-great-grandfather's treasure. As all of you know, this treasure is for our town, no matter how much is inside. Ready?"

"Open it, Amy," someone called. "I can't take the suspense any longer."

Laughter filled the room.

"Me, either," she said. "Reed, can you get this thing open?"

Using a screwdriver, Reed pried the lock from the box. "There you go. It's all yours."

With shaky fingers, she lifted the lid. The crowd pressed in, necks straining to see inside.

"What is it, Amy? How rich are we?"

Puzzled, she reached inside and withdrew a fragile, yellowed sheet of paper. "It's a letter."

"What else? Gotta be some gold."

"Maybe the letter tells where the gold mine is," someone said, and heads nodded in agreement.

Amy carefully unfolded the fragile paper and read:

> "Dire times brought the content of this box to you. This is your treasure. In the finding, in the hoping, in the faith. Yours, Mack Tanner. September 5, 1898."

She looked up from the letter and saw her bewilderment reflected on the faces around her.

"I don't get it," someone said. "What does he mean? Where's the gold?"

"Maybe there is no gold," Harry said.

"No gold?" A few voices began to grumble.

Reed spoke up. "Wait a minute, folks. I think I understand the message old Mack Tanner wanted to send. During the last year, this little town has struggled. But when times were hardest, we didn't crumble. With God's help and a lot of hope, we've pulled together. With faith and hope, we'll make it through this recession as a town, and be stronger for it in the end. And that's more valuable than all the gold in the Klondike."

Moved, Amy slipped her hand into Reed's. Reed, more than anyone, understood the value of friends, and a town that went the extra mile. Without her guides searching through the freezing night, he would have died in that shack.

"Reed is right," she said. "The spirit of Christmas—this beautiful spirit that filled the sanctuary tonight—will remain alive and well in Treasure Creek as long as we focus on what really matters. During the past year, we've learned some valuable lessons. I know *I* have. When Ben died, you were there for me. When my boys were kidnapped, this town—" she paused to point around the room "—you and you and you were there, caring, searching, shoving coffee into my hands, giving me hugs and prayers. And when Reed was injured, the love and determination of friends in this little town saved him." Emotion clogged the back of her throat, but she went on. "Life is not about riches. Life is about hope and faith and love, the greatest gifts of all. And here in Treasure Creek we have those gifts in abundance."

Slowly, the bewilderment changed to smiles. "We got each other. That's what matters."

"Yeah."

"That's right."

"Praise the Lord."

Amy's eyes filled at her town's reaction to what could have been a disappointing moment. They were amazing, these strong, resilient Alaskans.

She'd badly wanted to give them the financial answer to their prayers, but their reaction to the chest's contents was better than all the riches of the earth.

The spirit of Christmas *had* been alive and well in Treasure Creek since the problems began. This was the true treasure and the true meaning of Christmas. With God's help, they'd stayed together as a town, and He, not Amy James and not Mack Tanner, would see them through this financial crisis.

Jake, who'd been standing next to her, eyebrows drawn together in thought, said, "Mind if I have a look at that?"

"At what?"

"The box. There's something else in there, Amy. Below the lining. See it sticking up?"

Amy tilted the small, oddly empty chest toward the oilman. He reached inside and withdrew another yellow sheet. This one bore an elaborate heading and an official seal.

"What it is, Jake?"

He read for a moment, and the frown between his eyes was slowly replaced by wonderment. "It's a deed. A warranty deed."

The crowd pressed closer, murmuring at the announcement.

"Is it the gold mine?" someone asked.

Amy pulled at Jake's wrist, tilting the page so she could read. "It's a land deed, a legal description, isn't it?"

Jake rattled off the legal mumbo jumbo about county, section, plot.

"It's the deed to a piece of property. Seems old Mack Tanner left you something tangible after all." He began to smile. "For years, my company has been trying to find the legal deed to this piece of land. People, Amy's right about the real treasure being inside us, but I also believe I hold in my hands the solution to the town's financial worries."

"There's lots of land around here, Jake," Nate said. "Even if we find a buyer, the price won't be that much, will it?"

"You're not selling this land. Ever. You're going to reap the benefits of what it has to offer."

"What, Jake? Tell us." Amy's pulse beat with renewed hope in the monetary value of the treasure.

"A different kind of gold. Black gold."

"Oil?" Casey gasped, moving next to her man. "Jake, are you serious? There's oil on that property?"

"If I'm right, there could be enough oil beneath this property to keep Treasure Creek thriving for years. I can't say for sure, but it looks good." He laughed. "It looks real good."

Epilogue

Amy, Reed, Dexter, Sammy and Granny celebrated a joyous Christmas filled with love and laughter, and if there were a few poignant memories tossed in, that was to be expected. Remembering Ben was a good thing, now that Reed was no longer plagued by guilt. Fact of the matter, Reed figured it was the best Christmas he'd ever spent.

Rather than his usual solitary cup of coffee by the fireplace before heading off to work, Reed had been awakened by two overexcited boys yelling, "Come on, Chief. It's Christmas. Get up."

The scent of coffee and cinnamon in his nostrils, he levered one eye up just as Sammy dove onto the bed and wrapped his small arms around Reed's neck. They might as well be wrapped around his heart, too.

He'd made a growling sound. "Come here, you two scoundrels."

The wiggling, giggling pair plowed beneath the lifted covers for a wrestling match. So what if they bumped his sore leg and made him wince a time or two. They were worth the pain.

He'd never imagined how two little boys and one small

woman could change his humdrum life from routine duty to unpredictable fulfillment. One morning, while he'd been recovering from the gunshots, he awakened to find Dexter lying beside him, reading a storybook. Another time, Sammy had been sitting on his chest studying his whiskers. They had disorganized his entire life. And he loved them for it.

For years he'd spent Christmas working or alone in front of the television. But not this one.

By the time he and the boys had made their way into the living room, Amy was there, the fire was crackling, and his coffee and thick slices of pumpkin bread waited on the end table. Christmas carols played softly from the stereo and the lights on the tree flashed cheerful colors. Amy had placed a nativity set on the mantel and the holy family seemed to glow with the same peace and love he was feeling.

Amy smiled. "Merry Christmas."

His insides went crazy as they did every time he thought of spending a new day with Amy. He crossed the room, grinning as she maneuvered toward the doorway and a dangling piece of mistletoe. Face tilted upward, she received his kiss with a happy hum.

"Now that's the way to start the day," she said.

Reed agreed, so he kissed her again.

Granny Crisp, in a heavy robe and thermal socks, bustled in from the kitchen, waving a wooden spoon. "Well, are we gonna open gifts or spend all day lollygagging under the mistletoe? I got a turkey to cook, you know."

The mistletoe was fine with Reed, but Sammy and Dexter dove beneath the tree with a shout of glee. Pretty paper ripped and crackled. Small voices gasped in excitement and whooped with pleasure. Reed pulled an ottoman close to the tree and sat down to watch, his coffee cup in hand. He'd overindulged them, he feared, but what did he know? He'd never been a father-to-be before.

When the boys' gifts were opened and the toy train choo-chooed around the track, Amy handed out the adults' gifts. Granny got misty-eyed, a rare occurrence, when she opened the beautiful engraved Bible Amy bought her. Flustered, she wiped her face with the hem of her robe and scurried into the kitchen, taking the gift with her.

Amy and Reed exchanged glances. "I think she likes it."

They exchanged their own gifts then. A pair of funny socks and new boots for him. An engagement ring for her. After she finally stopped crying, he held her in his arms and kissed her until she promised to marry him on New Year's Eve.

Sammy and Dexter added kisses and drawings to Ben's stocking, and filled Reed's with little gifts and candies that made his heart dance. He'd never been loved with such completeness. Amy and the boys made him whole.

Amy claimed she felt the same, and from the look in her eyes and the dozens of kisses she stole beneath the mistletoe, Reed knew she spoke the truth. He still didn't know why God had chosen to bless him this way, but he wasn't about to argue.

So the day had gone, joyous and fulfilling and sweet, with old memories and new ones. Reed couldn't imagine life would ever get better than this.

Happily, he was wrong.

New Year's Eve was cold and clear and dark as pitch. No one inside the school gymnasium gave a thought to the weather, though, least of all Amy.

Tonight she had married the one her heart loved. Tonight she had become Mrs. Reed Truscott.

She looped an arm through her new husband's elbow as they made their way down the aisle toward the opposite end, where the bride's and groom's tables waited. Sammy and Dexter, dressed in the cutest little tuxedoes, skipped along beside, with Cy happily trailing the pair.

They'd invited the whole town, and from the look of the school gymnasium, the only building large enough for such a celebration, most of Treasure Creek had come to the combination wedding and New Year's Eve celebration.

Bethany had outdone herself in putting together the wedding on such short notice. She'd transformed the gym into a festive hall, with a flowered altar and pillars, and gauzy tulle on one end, where Pastor Ed had performed the vows. Tables laden with wedding cake and catered food waited on the other.

In between were the guest chairs that could be removed later if anyone wanted to dance in the New Year. Overhead, hundreds of balloons and confetti waited for the midnight drop.

Along the trail of flower petals, the newlyweds stopped numerous times for hugs and congratulations.

Amy paused next to Gage and Karenna Parker. Next to them sat Karenna's cousin Maryanne with husband, Alex Havens, beaming at each other with the same look they'd had at their wedding a short time ago.

"The songs were beautiful, Karenna. Thank you for singing."

"My pleasure." Karenna held little Matthew on her lap. She handed the boy to her handsome husband and stood, leaning across to embrace Amy.

Before she could sit down, Gage said, "Did Karenna tell you the news?" A wide grin creased his features. His dark eyes gleamed with pride. He glanced down at Karenna and she smiled. "I haven't told them."

"Told us what?" But from their secret, loving looks, Amy suspected the truth.

"We're going to have a baby."

Reed and Gage shook hands, thumping backs in that male manner of expressing emotion. Amy squealed and hugged her good friend. "I'm so happy for you."

"Maybe you and Reed will have the same news this time next year," Karenna suggested, arching her pretty eyebrows.

Amy laughed, but the idea didn't upset her one bit. A little boy who looked like Reed? Or maybe a girl this time, with Reed's dark hair and eyes? Her pulse fluttered to think of the possibility.

Reed must have been thinking the same thing, because he leaned down and kissed her for the tenth time in ten minutes. "A baby, huh?"

Smiling, Amy rubbed her nose against his, then took his hand and they moved on to take their position behind the cake table. Casey and Jake, who'd served as honor attendants, came, too, to make the appropriate toasts.

As the traditional speeches were given, Amy looked out across the gathered friends and family. Bethany had stopped working to lean against Nate McMann and watch the cake-cutting. It wouldn't be long until the pair of them was married, too. Penelope Lear and Tucker Lawson were there, as well. Penelope sported a diamond big enough to replace the moon. And across the room, completely lost in each other's eyes, were Harry Peterson and Joleen Jones.

The only person missing was Delilah. She had flown to Las Vegas with Ronald on Christmas Day, and that night, she'd called to say they'd been married. Amy had laughed in delight to hear her friend's happy voice.

And so the reception commenced, with toasts and kisses and music and food.

At five until midnight, Jake Rodgers wrestled the microphone from Ethan Eckles, a surprisingly good deejay. Casey stood at his side, looking beautiful in her blue satin gown. Gone were the cargo pants and unisex shirts, in honor of Amy's wedding. Before too long, Amy would return the favor at Casey and Jake's wedding.

"I have an announcement to make," Jake said, and the PA squealed. He jerked, holding the mike away from his face. "Maybe I don't."

The crowd laughed, then quieted. Jake had already shared the news with Amy and Reed, and they'd asked him to make the announcement tonight, when most of the town would be present.

"I guess all of you heard about the deed we found in Amy's treasure chest. Well, I was right." He stopped to grin. "I love being right. Treasure Creek now owns the deed to a fortune in oil. Happy New Year, everyone."

A cheer went up. Ethan took the microphone and started the countdown to midnight. The gym rocked with the sound of happy revelers joining the fray.

"Three, two, *one!*"

Someone released the balloons and Ethan kicked on the stereo, spinning the familiar "Auld Lang Syne."

Amy threw her arms around her new husband. "Happy New Year!"

Reed tugged her close for their first kiss of the New Year, but certain not to be the last. "Happy forever."

With balloons and confetti falling around them, and music swelling in their ears and the love and support of an entire town, Amy let the truth of his words settle into her heart.

Tonight was not just the beginning of a New Year or a new marriage, it was the beginning of forever.

Here in Treasure Creek, Alaska, the little town that could and did, she and her true love had found each other. Together with their boys, they would forge a life that, like

Mack Tanner's, would impact the future in a good and blessed way.

With God as their one true guide, their adventure had just begun.

And that was the greatest treasure of all.

* * * * *

Dear Reader,

Thank you for reading this final book in the Alaskan Bride Rush continuity, *The Lawman's Christmas Wish.* I love writing Christmas books, and I've always been fascinated with Alaska and the rugged individualists who make their home there. So, when the editors at Steeple Hill asked me to be a part of this series, I jumped at the opportunity. Now I'm a little sad to leave these characters behind. I hope you feel the same.

Like Amy and Reed and the rest of Treasure Creek, I pray this season finds you basking in the true meaning of Christmas. May hope and faith and love, and the Prince of Peace, guide you into a wonderful Christmas and a happy New Year.

I love hearing from readers. You may contact me at Steeple Hill, 233 Broadway, Ste. 1001, New York, NY 10279, or through my website at www.lindagoodnight.com.

Merry Christmas!

Linda Goodnight

QUESTIONS FOR DISCUSSION

1. Who was your favorite character in *The Lawman's Christmas Wish*. Why?

2. Describe the setting of Treasure Creek and how the rugged Alaskan terrain plays a part of the story.

3. The spiritual message of this book is subtle. What do you think it is? Why?

4. Though Amy James is only thirty-two, she feels responsible for the whole town. Why? Do you think she is justified in this feeling?

5. Could or would Treasure Creek have survived without Amy's persistence? Discuss and then defend your answer.

6. Amy receives several marriage proposals, most out of kindness to a young widow. How do you feel about marrying for reasons other than love? Compare the customs of marriage in biblical times and in other societies with that of America and others in the Western world.

7. Amy does things out of love. Reed does them out of duty. How does this difference cause conflict between them? How does it keep them apart?

8. Reed struggles with an overactive sense of responsibility. Do you think his father had anything to do with this? If so, what? How did his father treat him?

9. Many people like Reed have trouble relating to God as a loving father, and instead see God as an angry or indifferent judge. Which way do you view God? What does Jesus teach about who God is?

10. Both Amy and Reed must change in order to find each other. How does each change? Who changes the most?

11. Dexter and Sammy, Amy's sons, grieve for their dead father. Reed suggests they hang a Christmas stocking for him and put their love in it. Do you think he handled the situation properly? Can you think of other ways to help a grieving child at Christmas?

12. Mack Tanner's treasure chest at first appears to contain only a letter. How did you feel about that discovery? Were you disappointed, as some of the townspeople were? Which treasure do you think was best? The love and commitment of the town working together? Or the oil-rich land deed?

13. Was there any part of the story you would change if you could? If so, what was it and how would you change it?

14. Delilah Carrington came to Treasure Creek as a shallow husband hunter. How did she change? What changed her? Do you think she is mature enough in the end to make a lasting marriage with Ronald?

15. In the beginning of the book, Reed is sometimes gruff and short with Amy. Why do you think he behaves this way? Do you think he's always cared for her? Or is the emotion new and uncomfortable?

TITLES AVAILABLE NEXT MONTH

Available December 28, 2010

HIS COUNTRY GIRL
The Granger Family Ranch
Jillian Hart

THE BABY PROMISE
Carolyne Aarsen

THE COWBOY'S FAMILY
Brenda Minton

SECOND CHANCE RANCH
Leann Harris

THE RANCHER'S REUNION
Tina Radcliffe

ROCKY MOUNTAIN HERO
Audra Harders

REQUEST YOUR FREE BOOKS!

2 FREE INSPIRATIONAL NOVELS PLUS 2 FREE MYSTERY GIFTS

YES! Please send me 2 FREE Love Inspired® novels and my 2 FREE mystery gifts (gifts are worth about $10). After receiving them, if I don't wish to receive any more books, I can return the shipping statement marked "cancel." If I don't cancel, I will receive 6 brand-new novels every month and be billed just $4.24 per book in the U.S. or $4.74 per book in Canada. That's a saving of over 20% off the cover price. It's quite a bargain! Shipping and handling is just 50¢ per book.* I understand that accepting the 2 free books and gifts places me under no obligation to buy anything. I can always return a shipment and cancel at any time. Even if I never buy another book, the two free books and gifts are mine to keep forever.

105/305 IDN E7PP

Name (PLEASE PRINT)

Address Apt. #

City State/Prov. Zip/Postal Code

Signature (if under 18, a parent or guardian must sign)

Mail to Steeple Hill Reader Service:

IN U.S.A.: P.O. Box 1867, Buffalo, NY 14240-1867
IN CANADA: P.O. Box 609, Fort Erie, Ontario L2A 5X3

Not valid for current subscribers to Love Inspired books.

Want to try two free books from another series? Call 1-800-873-8635 or visit www.morefreebooks.com.

* Terms and prices subject to change without notice. Prices do not include applicable taxes. N.Y. residents add applicable sales tax. Canadian residents will be charged applicable provincial taxes and GST. Offer not valid in Quebec. This offer is limited to one order per household. All orders subject to approval. Credit or debit balances in a customer's account(s) may be offset by any other outstanding balance owed by or to the customer. Please allow 4 to 6 weeks for delivery. Offer available while quantities last.

Your Privacy: Steeple Hill Books is committed to protecting your privacy. Our Privacy Policy is available online at www.SteepleHill.com or upon request from the Reader Service. From time to time we make our lists of customers available to reputable third parties who may have a product or service of interest to you. If you would prefer we not share your name and address, please check here. ☐

Help us get it right—We strive for accurate, respectful and relevant communications. To clarify or modify your communication preferences, visit us at www.ReaderService.com/consumerschoice.

LIREG10R

When Texas Ranger Benjamin Fritz arrives at his captain's house after receiving an urgent message, he finds him murdered and the man's daughter in shock.

Read on for a sneak peek at DAUGHTER OF TEXAS by Terri Reed, the first book in the exciting new TEXAS RANGER JUSTICE *series, available January 2011 from Love Inspired Suspense.*

Corinna's dark hair had loosened from her normally severe bun. And her dark eyes were glassy as she stared off into space. Taking her shoulders in his hands, Ben pulled her to her feet. She didn't resist. He figured shock was setting in.

When she turned to face him, his heart contracted painfully in his chest. "You're hurt!"

She didn't seem to hear him.

Blood seeped from a scrape on her right upper biceps. He inspected the wound. Looked as if a bullet had grazed her. Whoever had killed her father had tried to kill her. With aching ferocity, rage roared through Ben. The heat of the bullet cauterized the flesh. It would probably heal quickly enough.

But Ben had a feeling that her heart wouldn't heal anytime soon. She'd adored her father. That had been apparent from the moment Ben set foot in the Pike world. She'd barely tolerated Ben from the get-go, with her icy stares and brusque manner, making it clear she thought him not good enough to be in her world. But when it came to her father...

Greg had known that if anything happened to him, she'd need help coping with the loss.

Ben, I need you to promise me if anything ever happens to me, you'll watch out for Corinna. She'll need an anchor.

I fear she's too fragile to suffer another death.

Of course Ben had promised. Though he'd refused to even allow the thought to form that any harm would befall his mentor and friend. He'd wanted to believe Greg was indestructible. But he wasn't. None of them were.

The Rangers were human and very mortal, performing a risky job that put their lives on the line every day.

Never before had Ben been so acutely aware of that fact.

Now his captain was gone. It was up to him not only to bring Greg's murderer to justice, but to protect and help Corinna Pike.

For more of this story, look for DAUGHTER OF TEXAS by Terri Reed, available in January 2011 from Love Inspired Suspense.

Copyright © 2011 by Terri Reed

SHLISEXP0111

Love Inspired® SUSPENSE
RIVETING INSPIRATIONAL ROMANCE

Keeping the Lone Star State safe

Follow the men and women of the Texas Rangers,
as they risk their lives to help save others,
with

DAUGHTER OF TEXAS by **Terri Reed**
January 2011

BODY OF EVIDENCE by **Lenora Worth**
February 2011

FACE OF DANGER by **Valerie Hansen**
March 2011

TRAIL OF LIES by **Margaret Daley**
April 2011

THREAT OF EXPOSURE by **Lynette Eason**
May 2011

OUT OF TIME by **Shirlee McCoy**
June 2011

Available wherever books are sold.

Steeple Hill®

www.SteepleHill.com

LISCONT11

Love Inspired HISTORICAL

INSPIRATIONAL HISTORICAL ROMANCE

When Jenny Archibald lost her best friend, Lena, to a fever, she was determined to keep Lena's two-year-old daughter, Meggie, safe—and that meant taking the child to her uncle in Dakota Territory. She never expected to lose her heart to the young girl...or to Burke Edwards, Meggie's handsome uncle.

Look for

Dakota Father

by

LINDA FORD

Available in January wherever books are sold.

www.SteepleHill.com

Steeple Hill®

LIH82852